Bolan knew their haven was about to become a battlefield

"Do your people have any weapons?" he asked the village chief.

"Some of us have rifles for hunting," Adan replied. "But we came here to get away from the fighting, not to fight even more. We are not soldiers."

"I understand," Bolan replied, "but you're going to have to fight this time, or you're all going to die. Zhinkovitch knows about your village now, and he knows that you've taken us in."

"We will hide you if Zhinkovitch comes back," Adan said.

"That won't save you. Zhinkovitch won't rest until you are under his control."

"I will discuss what you have said with the village council," the chief said, "but I must tell you that I will vote for peace myself."

"That'll be a vote for slavery, then," the Executioner replied, "not peace. Can I talk to the council myself? If they decide to fight, I will stay here to help organize your men. If they decide not to fight, we will leave immediately, so as not to make things any worse for you."

The chief nodded his consent. "We have been cut off from the outside world for a long time. Maybe we need to hear the words of an outsider."

MACK BOLAN ®

The Executioner

DON PENDLETON'S
EXECUTIONER®
THE
FIGHT OR DIE

A GOLD EAGLE BOOK FROM
W⦿RLDWIDE.®

TORONTO • NEW YORK • LONDON
AMSTERDAM • PARIS • SYDNEY • HAMBURG
STOCKHOLM • ATHENS • TOKYO • MILAN
MADRID • WARSAW • BUDAPEST • AUCKLAND

First edition January 1997
ISBN 0-373-64217-2

Special thanks and acknowledgment to
Mike Kasner for his contribution to this work.

FIGHT OR DIE

I would define true courage to be a perfect sensibility of the measure of danger, and a mental willingness to incur it.

—W. T. Sherman: *Personal Memoirs*, II xxv, 1875

It takes a brave man to become a soldier, and it takes an even braver man to admit he's sometimes afraid. War isn't noble—people are.

—Mack Bolan

THE
MACK BOLAN®
LEGEND

Nothing less than a war could have fashioned the destiny of the man called Mack Bolan. Bolan earned the Executioner title in the jungle hell of Vietnam.

But this soldier also wore another name—Sergeant Mercy. He was so tagged because of the compassion he showed to wounded comrades-in-arms and Vietnamese civilians.

Mack Bolan's second tour of duty ended prematurely when he was given emergency leave to return home and bury his family, victims of the Mob. Then he declared a one-man war against the Mafia.

He confronted the Families head-on from coast to coast, and soon a hope of victory began to appear. But Bolan had broken society's every rule. That same society started gunning for this elusive warrior—to no avail.

So Bolan was offered amnesty to work within the system against terrorism. This time, as an employee of Uncle Sam, Bolan became Colonel John Phoenix. With a command center at Stony Man Farm in Virginia, he and his new allies—Able Team and Phoenix Force—waged relentless war on a new adversary: the KGB.

But when his one true love, April Rose, died at the hands of the Soviet terror machine, Bolan severed all ties with Establishment authority.

Now, after a lengthy lone-wolf struggle and much soul-searching, the Executioner has agreed to enter an "arm's-length" alliance with his government once more, reserving the right to pursue personal missions in his Everlasting War.

1

Mack Bolan looked down at the war-ravaged city as the UN chartered Russian Ilyushin Il-76 transport jet banked to the right on its final approach to the Sarajevo international airport. Even from the air, the damage was apparent. What had once been the civic soccer stadium was now a cemetery with long rows of white grave markers, and shell-blasted ruins dotted the landscape.

The pilot brought the big jet down to a smooth landing and taxied to a parking spot on the tarmac. More than three years of repeated shelling from the Serb controlled hills overlooking the city had made a ragged patchwork of the runways and taxi strips.

Bolan grabbed his carryall and made his way to the forward cabin door and deplaned. A multilingual sign, with the blue-and-white UN insignia prominently displayed on the side of the building in front of him, told him where to go for passenger processing. Hefting his bag, he walked over to what in better times had been the Sarajevo international passenger terminal. The side of the building bore witness to the battles that had been fought for the airport. The masonry was pocked by shellfire and shrapnel, and had been hurriedly patched.

Inside the terminal, the UN World Health Organization documents identifying him as an official observer of the U.S. government were barely glanced at as the Bosnian customs officials waved him through passport control. Anyone who came in on the UN supply flights had already been cleared through so many checks that another one was almost a waste of time. Not many people tried to sneak into Sarajevo.

Bolan was walking through the empty passenger lounge when he heard a woman's voice call out. "Dr. Jordan?"

He turned and saw a well-dressed, dark-haired woman with a heart-shaped Slavic face and deep green eyes. She looked to be in her late twenties and had a trim, fit body.

"I'm Nina Petrova," the woman introduced herself, her hand outstretched. "I'm deeply honored to be working with you."

Bolan took her hand briefly. "You've reserved quarters for me?" he asked.

"Yes, Doctor," she replied. "At the King George Hotel. A car is waiting for us outside."

Bolan knew that if she had been able to procure a car in Sarajevo, she had to know her business. Even though a truce was in effect, very little motor fuel was getting to the city, and private cars were a rarity. "Good," he said. "Let's go there first."

THE KING GEORGE HOTEL in the center of Sarajevo had seen better days. Even so, the staff tried hard to uphold the standards that had made the once grand hotel a favorite stop for royalty and movie stars in between the world wars. A bellhop led Bolan and Petrova to a room on the second floor.

"I swept the room this morning," Petrova said as soon as the door had closed behind the bellhop. "It's clean. We can talk safely here."

"What are your orders regarding this mission?" Bolan got right to the point.

Petrova looked him full in the face. "My orders are to assist you in any way that I can without reservation. Until this operation is successfully concluded, I am to be under your sole command and authority. What you say, I will do."

Bolan was a bit surprised to hear her say that. Even though he had worked with several Russian RSV agents over the post-cold war years, rarely had there been a mission where the Russians had submitted to complete American control. On every joint operation, there had been a Moscow agenda that had to be contended with.

"What is Moscow's interest in this particular situation?" Bolan asked.

Petrova frowned. "I do not understand."

"As you know," he said, "I'm here to track down a missing Bosnian-born physician who's been living in America, and take him back to the States. Since this is purely an American situation, and really doesn't involve the Russians, I'm a little surprised at the level of your government's cooperation. To be honest, I didn't expect it."

"The Russian people are not your enemies any longer, Mr. Bolan," she said, using his real name. "It is in the best interests of both our governments that the world be made a safer place, so we will do everything we can to make this happen. In this case the return of your Dr. Frank Kubura is in both of our nations' interests."

She straightened to almost a position of attention. "And, as I said before, I am greatly honored to be working with a man of your reputation and experience."

"My name now is Dr. Richard Jordan," Bolan reminded her.

"That is so," she said, a smile playing at the corners of her mouth, "but I still know who you really are."

"When do I get to talk to the UN people?" Bolan asked.

"Not until tomorrow morning."

"What's wrong with today?" he said. "They were told that I was coming, and they know that I was manifested on today's supply plane."

"Even though you are here as a representative of your President, the UN people will make you wait so they can save face and keep you in your place," Petrova said.

The self-important impotence of the UN in the Bosnian war was an old story, as was its resistance to what they saw as American meddling in the situation. Although he was more than ready to start the mission, Bolan knew that he couldn't push too hard at this point. "I guess I'll have to wait, then," he said.

LATER THAT EVENING, Petrova broke out the maps she had of the target area, while Bolan dug into his bag and brought out the supplemental aerial photos Stony Man Farm had provided for him.

Bolan's mission was simple. Several months earlier, when it looked like the latest Bosnian cease-fire was going to hold, Dr. Frank Kubura, a prominent Bosnian-American physician, had taken a surgical team to treat casualties of the long civil war. While working at the UN hospital in Sarajevo, he had disappeared. Since Dr. Kubura was one of America's leading viral researchers, as well as a member of the President's national health advisory council, when he went missing, the President became concerned.

When the UN couldn't find Kubura, the President asked Hal Brognola to put the intelligence-gathering resources of Stony Man Farm to work to determine what had happened to him. When their information indicated that the doctor had been taken to the remote mountain camp of a renegade Serbian warlord, who had carved out a private enclave in the east where the three republics of Bosnia, Serbia and Croatia came together, Bolan was sent to get him back.

"First off," the Executioner said, "tell me what you know about Dushan Zhinkovitch."

Petrova slowly shook her head. "Zhinkovitch is a throwback to the bad old days before Tito," she said. "He is little more than a Serbian bandit living in the mountains where he preys on the weak and the helpless. He has been taking in deserters from the Serbian and Croatian national armies for quite some time now and has built up a sizable private army. He occupies an old castle in the region and is setting himself up as a self-styled king."

"Is he likely to let us in to talk to Kubura without trying to hold us hostage?"

"We think so. Our information is that he does not want to do anything right now that will bring him unwelcome attention from any of the major political factions or from the UN. He is building his forces and slowly incorporating more and more territory, but he is not yet strong enough to withstand a major move against him."

Bolan nodded. "Since I'm still fighting jet lag, I'm going to turn in early. We'll go over this again in detail after we see the UN people tomorrow."

Petrova took that as her cue to leave. "My room is right through that door," she said, pointing to a door leading to the adjoining suite. "If you need anything, just knock."

A HUNDRED TEN MILES from Sarajevo, a stone fortress stood on the top of a rocky crag in the mountains where the newly formed republics of

Bosnia, Croatia and Serbia came together. During the days of Tito's Yugoslavia, it had been an inaccessible backwater. Even now it was so far from the fighting around the major cities that it had almost been forgotten by the combatants. Presently it was the headquarters of a man who intended to control that remote part of the Balkans.

"How is Niksha doing?" a booming voice said from the doorway of the large wood-paneled room on the ground floor of the fortress.

Dr. Frank Kubura turned to face the Serbian warlord who had taken him prisoner. Dushan Zhinkovitch was a huge man, even by the standards of the mountain people. He was in his early forties, with a full black beard and easily stood six foot six.

The warlord walked over to the four-poster and smiled down at his teenaged son, who had suffered a severe leg fracture in a riding accident. Kubura had been kidnapped to be the boy's private physician. It wasn't what he had come to Bosnia to do, but since his kidnapping in Sarajevo a little more than a month ago, he'd had no choice. As Zhinkovitch had explained when he had been brought to the fortress, he had made enemies in Sarajevo and at least he would stay alive in the mountains. When he wasn't seeing to the boy, Kubura tended the other patients in Zhinkovitch's infirmary, mostly troops who had gotten injured in drunken brawls.

"Your son is fine," Kubura answered. "His leg may give him a little trouble in the future, but it isn't serious."

"Very good, Doctor, very good." Zhinkovitch smiled through his bushy beard. "My son will need two good legs to keep the land I am acquiring for him."

Kubura didn't try to tell the warlord that his dynastic dreams for his son would never come to fruition. As soon as the Serbs or Croats got their act together, they would take him down, just like they had taken down other would-be local dictators. The nation building that was going on had no room in it for petty tyrants and warlords.

The doctor understood that the Serb was a man of the mountains and thought as his ancestors had for hundreds of years. In this part of the Balkans, a new thought was as rare as peace. And, because of that, Kubura knew that his only chance to keep living was to do as he was told.

"Your son will heal," he said, "but I recommend that you get him a different horse, or maybe a mare until he learns how to ride."

The Serb laughed. "He will have a new horse," he promised, "but no son of mine will ride a mare. A real man rides only stallions."

Kubura shook his head and said nothing.

2

The building that housed the UN offices in Sarajevo was as battered as the rest of the city. Shellfire had punched holes in the masonry walls, and some of the windows were held together only by tape. The Sarajevo office of the World Health Organization occupied most of the building's second floor and, even though Bolan and Petrova had an appointment with the WHO director, they were kept waiting for over an hour.

When they were finally shown into the office of Hamadija Aladic, the Bosnian head of the WHO wasn't glad to see them. "I do not understand why you have come to Sarajevo, Dr. Jordan, and I do not know what we can do to help you."

"It's quite simple," Bolan explained. "I've come to find Dr. Frank Kubura, and I need the proper UN passes that will let me through the checkpoints so I can search for him."

"That is what the New York headquarters told me last week," Aladic replied. "But I still do not understand why you are doing this. Trying to find one man in a country like this is futile."

"Kubura is not only one of America's leading viral researchers, but he's also on the President's national health advisory team. When he went missing," Bolan said, looking directly at the WHO director, "and the UN authorities couldn't seem to find him, the President asked me to come here to try to find out what happened to him."

"We reported to your government," the official said, "that Dr. Kubura was working at the UN hospital here when he disappeared. Beyond that, we have not been able to come up with anything on him. But this is a war zone, you know. People disappear from here all the time."

Bolan knew when he was being sandbagged. "My understanding is that there are reports from the UN peacekeepers saying that Kubura is being held captive in the mountain camp of a renegade Serbian warlord named Dushan Zhinkovitch."

Aladic shrugged. "That might have been what was reported," he said, "but we at the WHO have no confirmation of that. As I said, we have no information about his whereabouts at all."

"You do know who Dushan Zhinkovitch is, don't you?"

Aladic spread his hands in a gesture of helplessness. "It is not possible for me to know every petty commander in a situation as confused as this. Along with the three national armies, there are many bands of freebooters and other mercenary troops. It is not my job to know who all their commanders are."

"According to my sources," Bolan said, "Zhinkovitch has carved out a private enclave east of here in the mountains and is gathering troops to extend his area of control."

"You are very well-informed for a medical doctor," Aladic said.

Bolan shrugged. "The information was given to me by the President," he replied. "He is anxious—"

"You've said that already," the Bosnian interrupted. "You and your President must realize that there is more at stake here than the life of one American doctor who should not have come here in the first place. His so-called mercy mission was not cleared through me, or I would never have given him permission to come here."

"Our understanding is that you desperately need all the trained medical personnel you can get. However, I'm not here to argue that point with you," Bolan said firmly. "I only want the passes so I can go about finding Dr. Kubura. When do I get the clearance I need?"

"You will have them today," Aladic snapped, "but that is all you will get from me. And if you go missing, no one will look for you. We do not have enough personnel to spare."

Bolan fixed his eyes on the WHO official. "I'm sure that as long as I have the proper UN papers, I won't have any problems."

"This is a very dangerous country, Doctor," Aladic warned.

Bolan smiled thinly. "So it seems."

ONCE THE ORDERS were given, it took a clerk only a few minutes to type up the forms Bolan needed to pass them through any UN checkpoint and hopefully through the checkpoints of the warring factions, as well.

"Do you have any idea why Aladic was so sticky?" Bolan asked when he and Petrova were back in the car.

"That's easy," she replied. "The good doctor is making a fortune selling UN medical supplies to the combatant forces. Over half of everything that is flown in here goes directly onto the black market and he gets a big cut of the proceeds."

Bolan knew that the black market was a fact of life in this part of the world, but he was surprised anyway. "Why does the UN allow that to happen?"

"Certain high-ranking UN officials are working with the Russian Mafia that handles the cargo, and they are being paid off, too."

"Do you think that Kubura might have stumbled onto this operation and was taken out so he wouldn't report it?"

"That is certainly a possibility," she said. "I think that he would have had to be blind not to have noticed what was going on, he was here long enough. But I think that he was kidnapped instead of being killed because he is a skilled doctor. Doctors are in such short supply here that they did not want to waste him."

Bolan smiled grimly. "So much for this being a simple locate and rescue operation."

"Nothing is simple here."

"I'm beginning to understand that."

As soon as the American and the Russian had left the UN building, Dr. Hamadija Aladic went to his private office and placed a phone call to a local number.

"This is Aladic," he said when the phone was answered. "We need to talk. Something has come up regarding Kubura. The American government has sent someone to look for him, and we have to make plans. I will be at the warehouse at eight o'clock tonight.''

When he hung up the phone, Aladic stared out of his office window. Dushan Zhinkovitch would have to be told immediately that the Americans had sent an agent to look for the doctor. Regardless of his credentials from the WHO headquarters in New York, Aladic knew that the man who called himself Dr. Richard Jordan wasn't a physician. His manner was that of a soldier.

Even though he knew that Zhinkovitch was a law unto himself in his mountain stronghold, Aladic would strongly advise the Serbian warlord to allow the phony doctor to leave unharmed after he talked to Kubura. It wouldn't do for him to disappear as well. That would only bring more investigators, which was the last thing any of them needed. Now that the truce was in place, more supplies were coming into Sarajevo, and it wasn't the time to have strangers asking awkward questions.

Their operation had worked well so far, syphoning off a percentage of everything that was flown in. But any operation was only as secure as its weakest link, and they had been forced to use too many weak links for lack of choice. As soon as more Russians could be infiltrated into Sarajevo, they could replace, and eliminate, some of those weaker Bosnian links to tighten their security.

For now, though, their best protection was to let the American do what he had come to do, then leave.

WHILE THERE WAS a U.S. consulate in Sarajevo, there had been no easy way for Bolan to bring weapons into the country. Considering his cover, trying to smuggle weapons and military equipment in through the diplomatic pouch would have been too risky. He would have to be outfitted and supplied by the Russians this time.

After leaving the UN building, Petrova drove Bolan to a small warehouse controlled by the RSV, the latest Russian incarnation of their state security agency. A broad-shouldered Russian met them and led them inside. Petrova pointed to crates stacked against the wall. "The weapons are in there. Take what you think we will need."

Bolan opened the crates and found a wide selection of Russian weapons, cleaned and ready for use. He chose a folding stock AKM and one of the new 7.62 mm PPS silenced pistols for himself. The PPS, nicknamed Vul, was a newly developed weapon that used a unique piston cartridge instead of a bulky silencer. The explosive gases were trapped inside the cartridge case when the internal piston launched the projectile down the short barrel, and there was no report. It was very short ranged, but the 7.62 mm hollowpoint bullet had good stopping power.

"Can you use an AKM?" Bolan asked Petrova. Even though he planned to go in alone after the doctor, he wanted her as an armed backup.

"Am I not a Russian?" She smiled. "I grew up knowing how to use one."

Bolan chose a second folding stock AKM and a 9 mm Makarov pistol for her, then loaded a supply of magazines for them. Since carrying weapons openly wouldn't fit in with his WHO cover, Bolan wrapped the weapons and ammunition in black plastic sheets and tied them into two bundles. Petrova gathered together supplies and camping equipment.

"We are going to change cars," Petrova said as they headed out of the rear door of the warehouse.

She led Bolan to a white Fiat two-door sedan. "It's not much, but it's reliable."

Twin UN flags were mounted on the vehicle's front fenders. Supposedly they would give them safe passage. To Bolan, however, the flags looked more like good aiming points for any gunman with an AK-47 or RPG rocket launcher.

"It's not a Chevy Blazer," he said eyeballing the small car, "but I'll take your word that it'll do."

Bolan tied the weapon packs to the underside of the car, then loaded the rest of their gear into the back. If everything went as planned, they would be gone no more than two days, but he liked to be prepared, anyway.

ONCE BOLAN AND PETROVA had passed through the UN checkpoint on the outskirts of Sarajevo, the Bosnian countryside became a combination of the pastoral and the desolate. Ruined farmhouses stood beside overgrown gardens, and sheep grazed beside the burned out hulks of trucks and armored personnel carriers.

It was just over a hundred miles to Zhinkovitch's stronghold, but most of the roads were narrow and badly potholed.

"I was born and raised here," Petrova said. "My father was an army officer stationed at the Soviet consulate in Belgrade, and my Serb mother was a dancer with the state ballet."

"You speak the local languages then?"

"The Serbian and Croatian dialects I speak well," she said. "My Bosnian is not very good, but I can manage."

"You'd better be able to," Bolan said. "All I have is a little Russian."

"Russian works well in most cities," she replied, "but the country people do not like to speak it."

"Do you blame them?"

"Not really. Even though they were backing Tito, the Russians have never been well liked here."

"I'm not surprised," Bolan said dryly.

IT WAS LATE AFTERNOON when they hit the first of Zhinkovitch's checkpoints at the base of the hills, some twenty miles from his reported stronghold. Petrova slowed when they spotted troops manning a barricade across the dirt road.

"Drive normally," Bolan said. "According to our papers, we're part of the UN."

"Some of these people would even shoot at the Pope," Petrova replied.

3

Petrova brought the Fiat to a stop in front of the barricade and killed the engine. She rolled down the window as half a dozen gunmen with assault rifles surrounded the car. The men were dressed in a mixture of camouflage uniforms originally from several armies. The only uniform item they had in common was a black beret with a yellow crest on the front.

The man who looked to be in charge barked out a command, and Petrova turned to Bolan. "He says he wants to search us for weapons."

"Tell him that we are here under UN auspices," Bolan answered, "and that we have passes that allow us to go through without inspection."

The guard spoke again as he snapped down the muzzle of his AK-47 to center on Bolan's chest. "He says that he does not care if we are here under God's personal protection. His men will search us or we will not pass," Petrova translated.

Bolan was careful to keep his hands in sight and move slowly as he opened his door. "I guess we'd better let them search us then."

Petrova's eyes told Bolan that the guard's hands were doing more than merely patting her down for hardware. But since there was nothing he could do to help her that wouldn't endanger them both, Bolan knew that it would be best if he pretended not to notice the molestation. With the weapons hidden, the last thing he needed was a confrontation.

When the search was completed, the guard stood back and slung his AK-47 as he spoke to Petrova.

"He says that we are to follow their jeep," she reported. "We are not to stop anywhere unless they do. If we do, he says they will kill us."

As Petrova opened the driver's door of the Fiat, the guard leaned forward and whispered something in her ear. Then, with a barking laugh, he straightened and walked off.

"That filthy pig," Petrova snapped as she got into the vehicle.

"What did he say?"

"He said that he will be waiting for me when I come back this way. That if Zhinkovitch leaves anything, he will be glad to take it himself."

"If we come back this way," Bolan said, "I can assure you that he'll wish he had never seen you."

"Thank you," she replied with a thin smile, "but there is no need to trouble yourself. I can handle him myself."

"It would be no trouble at all," Bolan replied. "In fact I'd rather enjoy it."

"Maybe I will let you have what is left when *I* am done with him."

"That's fair."

THE TRIP TOOK almost an hour through increasingly mountainous terrain. The Russian-built GAZ jeep they followed had to have been running on three cylinders, because the Fiat had no trouble keeping up with it even on the steepest grades.

"There it is," Bolan said, pointing to an outcropping rising above the mountain in front of them. Perched in the outcropping was a stone fortress that had to date back to the days of the Turkish invaders. The last five hundred yards of the road up to the fortress hadn't been designed for motor vehicles. It had been widened from a narrow horse track, so that small trucks and four-wheel-drive vehicles could negotiate the switchbacks, but the drivers had to have nerves of steel. One side of the road was a solid rock face, and the other was a sheer drop-off. Under icy conditions, the road would be suicidal.

The road ended in a wooden bridge that spanned a moat. A massive stone gate was set into the wall, with watchtowers on either side, and thick wooden doors that stood open. The GAZ jeep drove into a cobblestoned courtyard, and Petrova pulled the Fiat up next to it and killed the engine.

A black-bearded bear of a man was waiting for them. He was dressed in a white gypsy shirt with an embroidered vest and black pants with the cuffs tucked into black boots. A curved dagger in a silver sheath was stuck into one side of his sash and a Russian 9 mm Makarov pistol into the other.

"That's him," Petrova said. "Dushan Zhinkovitch."

"I give welcome to my friends from the United Nations," Zhinkovitch said in heavily accented English as his arms waved them out of the car. "Come into my home."

Bolan stepped out into the courtyard. He could tell that the fortress's thick stone walls would withstand a lot of battering, even from high explosives. He noticed that the battlements were equipped with modern weapons and that heavy machine guns, rocket-propelled grenade launchers and recoilless rifles were placed behind sandbag-reinforced positions. He didn't want to seem too interested in the weapons and so alert Zhinkovitch, but he filed the defenses in his mind.

Flanked by three of his men, Zhinkovitch led Bolan and Petrova into a grand hall inside the main building. The high stone walls were covered with tapestries and banners, and long wooden tables were set in front of the walk-in fireplace.

The warlord led them to the head table and motioned them to two chairs set across the table from what looked like a throne.

"Sit," Zhinkovitch said as he settled into his carved chair. "I have food and drink for you after your long journey."

"We don't have much time," Bolan said. "We need to be back in Sarajevo before dark."

"But you must refresh yourselves with something," Zhinkovitch insisted. "I would be a bad host otherwise."

The warlord motioned toward the back of the hall, and three women walked in bearing plates of food and bottles of the local brandy. Bolan studied Zhinkovitch's eyes. They were flat and cold, devoid of human expression. He knew that if he needed to kill this man, he would have to do it quickly because the Serbian wouldn't die easily.

"So tell me," Zhinkovitch said, his dark eyes focused on Bolan, "what has brought you to my land?"

"My President has asked me to try to locate Dr. Frank Kubura," Bolan replied. "I've been informed that he's here with you. If that is so, I'm to take him back with me. Dr. Kubura is an important man in my government, and the President needs him."

Zhinkovitch looked at Bolan for a long moment before speaking. "He is here," he admitted, "but I do not understand why you want to take him away from me. You have many doctors in your country, but I have only him. It is not possible for him to go back to America with you."

"Why not?"

"Dr. Kubura has found much work to do here. Even though he lived in your country, he is of my people and he sees his duty to them."

"I'd like to talk to him about this myself."

"But of course." The warlord pushed back his chair. "We will go see him right now, and he will tell you this for himself."

ZHINKOVITCH'S INFIRMARY was in a basement room under the battlements. A dozen narrow beds flanked the walls and were lighted by a single naked bulb hanging from a wooden beam in the roof.

A man in a stained white coat and in need of a shave was standing by a patient's bed, taking the man's pulse. He looked up when the door opened.

"Dr. Kubura?" Bolan stepped forward. "I am Richard Jordan. The President sent me to talk to you. He wants you to return to the States with me."

Kubura appeared stunned. "I don't know what to say...."

"Doctor," Zhinkovitch said, "tell your friends that you wish to stay here with us."

Kubura's eyes flitted to the foot of the bed where one of Zhinkovitch's gunmen stood. The patient in the bed was a young Bosnian girl who had broken both her legs jumping from a second-story window to escape being raped. Given time her bones would mend, but he couldn't adequately control her pain because all the morphine was reserved for Zhinkovitch's troops.

He turned to Bolan. "I must stay here," he said dully. "I am a doctor and my patients need me."

Bolan looked at him for a long time. It was apparent that Kubura was being coerced. But there wasn't anything he could do about it right now. "If that's what you want me to tell the President," he told the doctor, "I will."

"Give him my thanks for his concern, but this is how it has to be."

"Now that this had been taken care of," Zhinkovitch said, fixing Bolan with his dark eyes, "you can go home to your President.

"But you," he said, turning to Petrova, "will stay here to assist Dr. Kubura."

"She goes back with me," Bolan stated, stepping forward.

"No," Zhinkovitch replied as his guards snapped down their AK-47s to cover Bolan. "I have many sick men here, and the doctor needs an assistant. It is too much work for one man. She will help him so they will get better faster."

Petrova looked at Bolan, then nodded toward the door. He stared at her for a long moment, then turned to go. He had no other choice.

The armed guard by the door led Bolan out to the courtyard where he saw that the Fiat had been turned around, its engine running. A guard with an AK-47 at the ready stood by the open driver's door, while another armed guard sat in the back seat. Zhinkovitch wasn't taking any chances.

Bolan opened the passenger-side door and slid in.

"Come back whenever you want, Doctor." The Serbian's laughter rolled over the sound of the idling engines. "I can always use another doctor."

Dropping the Fiat into first gear, the Serbian driver led the men in the GAZ jeep through the main gate. Bolan didn't turn around and look at Petrova as he left. He knew it would be better if he didn't.

ZHINKOVITCH RETURNED to the infirmary and found Dr. Kubura tending to his youngest patient.

"You like this little one, don't you?" the Serb said. "Maybe you think that when she gets better, you can have her?"

Kubura shook his head. "She is a patient," he replied wearily, "and I am her doctor. I'm just trying to heal what your men did to her."

Drawing the dagger from the sash around his waist, Zhinkovitch leaned over the girl. "She is very pretty, but she is not as pretty as the Russian nurse I got for you. Maybe it would be better if you did not have to worry about this one anymore.''

"No!" Kubura yelled as he lunged for the Serb leader, but one of the guards held him back.

The curved edge of the dagger flashed as it sliced into the flesh of the girl's throat. Blood spurted briefly. She was dead in an instant.

Kubura slumped against the guard's grip. He was a doctor, a healer, but for the first time, he wanted to kill someone.

4

"You should thank me for doing that, Doctor," Zhinkovitch said as he wiped the blade clean. "Now you can devote all your attention to my son and my men."

"You're going to pay for that," Kubura said, his voice shaking with helpless rage.

Zhinkovitch looked at him with the trace of a smile on his broad face. "And who is going to make me pay, little man? You? You are a doctor, and doctors do not make war on men like me. Or do you think your God will punish me in the afterlife? God may still be alive in your country, but he has long since left here."

That was a fact, Kubura thought bitterly.

"I can do anything I like," Zhinkovitch went on. "There is no one to stop me. While those fools down there—" he gestured toward the valley "—fight their stupid battles for power, I am the power up here in the mountains. I am like a god to these people. I am the one who says who lives and who dies.

"When they have finished killing one another down there, I will move in and be the power there as well. Everyone will know the name of Dushan Zhinkovitch. And before you think about doing something stupid, Doctor," he cautioned, "remember that I have that Russian woman now. I would hate to see her hurt because you underestimated me."

"I won't underestimate you," Kubura said. "You have shown me what you are capable of."

"Just see that you never forget it."

Kubura's eyes flickered over to the bed where the dead girl lay. "I won't forget," he said. "You can be sure of that."

Zhinkovitch fixed him with a long gaze before turning on his heel and walking out.

NINA PETROVA KNEW that she was in over her head. The minute that Bolan had been driven away, two of Zhinkovitch's gunmen had taken her to a small room on the second floor of the main building. The room was paneled in carved wood, the floors were carpeted with handwoven antique rugs, and there was a huge four-poster covered with goose-down comforters. It wasn't

difficult for her to guess what her new role was
going to be.

The best she could hope for was that Zhinkovitch would keep her for himself and not share
her with his men. If Bolan could get back soon
enough, it might not be too long an ordeal. She
shuddered when she thought of being given to
the troops. She recalled her training as an intel-
ligence agent. Petrova knew that, short of death,
she could survive whatever happened. But more
than that, she wanted to keep it from happening
at all. She wasn't so sure, however, that she
would have much choice in the matter. She didn't
think that Zhinkovitch was the kind of man to
pay much attention to a woman's wishes.

Petrova wasn't from a privileged family, as
were so many of the RSV agents. Getting into
what had been the KGB had been done on the
power of her abilities. Her striking good looks
hadn't hurt either, and she had learned early on
to use all her assets to her advantage. The new era
of cooperation with the West had given her the
chance to put her language skills to work.

When the Russians wanted to keep tabs on
what was happening in the once-united Yugoslavia, her birthplace and native tongue made her
a natural for the position. Her cover was that of
a medical staff member at the Russian consul-

ate, which had given her wide access to the various warring factions as well as the UN agencies in Bosnia.

In her three years in Sarajevo, however, this was the first time that she had been in serious danger. It was ironic that she was being forced to depend on an American to free her, but Mack Bolan was probably the best man to have on her side.

IT WAS LATE AFTERNOON when Bolan's escort passed through Zhinkovitch's last checkpoint and stopped by the side of the road. When the driver and the man riding shotgun in the back seat got out of the Fiat, their leader aimed the muzzle of his AK-47 at Bolan.

"Go now," he said, "and do not come back."

"I'm going."

Bolan was careful to keep both of his hands in plain sight as he slid over to the driver's side. He slowly pulled onto the main road back to Sarajevo. In his rearview mirror, he saw the gunmen turn their Russian GAZ jeep and head back toward the fortress.

The Executioner drove on for another few miles before he came to a small village. Several of the houses were little more than bombed-out shells, but thin tendrils of smoke rose from the chimneys of a couple of them. When he saw a horse penned behind one of the buildings, he decided to stop.

All of the warlord's outposts would have been alerted to be on the lookout for a man in a white Fiat flying UN flags, but they might not be as concerned about a man on horseback.

THE SERBIAN GUNMEN at the checkpoint had just finished their evening meal when Bolan crept up behind the guard shack. They were focused on watching the road from Sarajevo in front of them rather than keeping a 360-degree watch. Failure to pay close attention to their surroundings was going to be their downfall.

It had been simple for Bolan to get back to a position overlooking the checkpoint. The owner of the horse had been more than willing to trade the animal for the Fiat. After removing the weapons from under the car, Bolan took out his night black combat suit, assault harness and boots, and changed.

He took one of the AKMs, the silenced pistol and the Makarov originally intended for Petrova and as much ammunition as he could comfortably carry. The other AKM he left with the farmer to buy his silence.

It had been dusk when he had set out and, as he had thought, no one had paid any attention to a man on horseback. He had kept watch on the guard shack for half an hour, making sure that he knew how many men were posted there, before turning the horse loose and moving in closer on foot.

A Serb soldier went behind the guard shack, his AK-47 held at the ready. When he passed within five yards of where Bolan was hiding, the warrior slipped the safety off the stubby Russian PPS silent pistol and steadied it in a two-handed grip aimed at the side of the guard's head. He hadn't had a chance to test fire the new weapon back in Sarajevo, but he had read the technical Intel reports on it that had come into Stony Man Farm. It should perform to standard.

The Serb turned and raised his weapon. The silenced Vul pistol spit, and the piston-launched 7.62 mm hollowpoint bullet exploded in his brain, scrambling his neural synapses. He fell facefirst without making a sound.

Bolan slipped through the shadows toward the guard shack. He wanted to do this as quietly as he could, but he knew that there was no way to do it fast enough with the silenced pistol. For one thing, shooting the soft, hollowpoint slugs through the window would throw off his aim. The glass wouldn't deflect the more powerful 7.62 mm AK rounds, though.

He extended the buttstock of his paratroop AKM and flicked the selector switch halfway down to semiauto fire. There was no sense in making any more noise than was absolutely necessary. There were five guards that he had to take care of now, and that meant five shots, six at the most, rather than bursts of full-auto fire.

Peering through the window, Bolan saw four of the guards, their weapons in their hands, but not the fifth man. He could take out those four from where he was, but he couldn't count on the missing man being asleep or not alert. As it was, he was going to have to storm the front door and hope that it gave him a better line of fire.

Flicking off the Makarov's safety, Bolan crept around to the front of the shack. The door was cracked open to provide ventilation against the coal stove burning in the center of the room, so he wouldn't have to kick open a lock. Taking a deep breath, he pushed against the edge of the door. It crashed wide open, and the Executioner went in with both weapons blazing.

The first three rounds struck true. The single AKM shot took out a Serb, and the Makarov put two quick 9 mm rounds into the man operating the radio. The two guards seated at the table brought up their weapons just in time to catch the next two AKM rounds that hammered them off their stools.

The fifth man who had been hidden from view lunged for the rifle on the end of his bunk. He was bringing it to bear when Bolan's thumb flicked the AKM fire selector to full-auto and he snapped off a 3-round burst. Two of the bullets connected and the man was slammed back against the wall of the hut, the AK-47 falling from his hands.

Catching movement from the corner of his eye, Bolan spun in time to see that one of the guards was only wounded and was aiming a pistol at him. Throwing himself to the floor, the Executioner rolled to bring his Makarov into play and triggered two snap shots as the Serb's rounds went over his head. The two 9 mm slugs drilled into the gunman's chest, one through his heart. The pistol fell from his nerveless fingers.

After making sure that the rest of the Serbs were dead, Bolan dropped the partially spent magazines from the AKM and the Makarov, replacing them with fresh ones. Spotting a crate of Russian hand grenades stacked against the wall, he helped himself to four of them and hooked them onto his assault harness.

As a precaution, he ripped the antenna lead out of the radio on the table. If Zhinkovitch was as organized as he appeared to be, there would probably be some kind of radio check with the guard post during the night. Bolan had to make his move as soon as possible. He also didn't want to leave the woman up there any longer than necessary.

He got into the GAZ jeep parked outside, switched on the ignition and hit the starter. Switching on the blackout lights, he drove out to the road and turned toward Zhinkovitch's fortress.

WHEN BOLAN REACHED the bottom of the narrow, twisting road that led to Zhinkovitch's stronghold, he pulled the vehicle off the road and parked it behind a nearby clump of trees. Gathering his weapons, he started up the hill.

Zhinkovitch hadn't sent patrols out to cover the approaches to his sanctuary. Though the fortress was perched on a rocky crag, it wasn't the kind of rock face that required specialized climbing gear to negotiate. A man wearing rubber-soled combat boots, as Bolan was, could easily make it to the top.

Slinging his AKM behind his back, he started to climb. Once he reached the wall itself, he found that the stones were irregular enough that he had no trouble making his way up to the battlements. Pressing himself against the face of the wall, Bolan looked through the gaps in the battlements and saw that the walkway was clear.

5

Slipping through the battlements, Bolan crouched in the shadow of the wall and took stock of his surroundings. Even though it was close to midnight, there was enough light from inside the fortress for him to take off his night-vision goggles and hook them on his assault harness. A sizable diesel generator chugged on the far side of the enclosure, loud enough to mask any sounds he might make.

He started down the walkway under the battlements. Hearing a muted cough from the machine-gun emplacement in front of him, he froze. Looking closer, he saw a guard leaning against the sandbags with his back to him.

Drawing his chisel-pointed Cold Steel Tanto fighting knife from its boot-top sheath, Bolan started forward and slipped up behind the Serb. Before the man could bring up his weapon, Bolan clamped his left hand over the guard's mouth and lower jaw as he snapped his head to the side.

At the same instant, he drove the razor-sharp blade into the hollow at the right side of the man's neck, severing both his carotid artery and jugular vein.

The guard's eyes flashed open and he reached to pull away from Bolan's iron grip, but the sudden loss of blood shut his brain down and he went limp. The smell of blood was strong as Bolan silently lowered the body to the walkway and rolled it against the base of the battlements.

He paused at the DshK-46 heavy machine gun in its sandbagged emplacement just long enough to strip the ammunition belt from the gun's breech. He didn't want to take the time to permanently disable the weapon, but at least the gunners would have to reload it, which would buy him a few seconds if he came back that way.

A few yards farther along, Bolan found the stone stairs leading to the cobblestoned courtyard below. With his back hugging the wall, he kept his eyes fixed on the courtyard as he made his way down. At the bottom of the stairs, he stuck to the shadows as he made his way around the walls to the keep's central building.

When a guard appeared from behind the portable generator, Bolan froze, his hand on the grip of the silenced pistol. But the guard continued on his way without looking into the shadows. He disappeared into one of the barracks buildings, and the big American dashed the last few yards to the steps leading into the great hall. There was no guard on the door, so he slipped through and saw that the corridor inside was clear as well.

Figuring that the lower floors contained the kitchens or storage rooms, he decided to check the upper floors first. If his assessment of Petrova's fate was right, the warlord would more than likely have taken her to the living quarters in the upper stories.

Peering around the corner at the top of the stairs, Bolan saw an armed guard sitting in a chair beside a carved wooden door. Since he was the only guard he had encountered in the building, the chances were good that that was where Petrova was being held. Either that or it was the warlord's bedroom, but that would work just as well.

Holding the silenced pistol in a two-handed grip, Bolan stepped out into the open and purposefully slammed the heel of his boot against the wall behind him. When the guard looked over at the sound, the Executioner shot him in the forehead. The Serb fell out of the chair with a thud, twitched once, then lay still.

PETROVA HEARD a slight sound at her door and stiffened. Her ordeal with Zhinkovitch was as bad as she had feared, but at least he had promised he would keep her for himself, so she didn't have to worry about being sent to the barracks to entertain the troops. The warlord had left satisfied, so she didn't know why he would be coming back now. She was stunned when she saw Bolan slip through the door with an AK-47 in his hand.

"Are you okay?" he asked as he placed the guard's rifle and magazine carrier on the bed beside her.

"Yes."

"Good. Get dressed. We're leaving."

Bolan walked over to the window while she dressed, as much to scope out an escape route as to give her privacy.

"I am ready," Petrova said.

"Do you know where Kubura sleeps?"

"Down in the infirmary, I think."

Opening the door a crack, Bolan made sure the coast was clear before grabbing the dead guard's arms and dragging him into the bedroom.

"Follow me," he told Petrova. They didn't encounter anyone else until they got down to the corridor leading to the infirmary. Bolan saw another guard sitting in front of the infirmary door.

This time, there was no way for him to get close enough to the guard to use his knife and, since the Serb was half hidden behind a pillar, he didn't have a clear shot for the silenced pistol, either.

"I want you to distract him," he whispered to Petrova. "Get him out in the open so I can get a clear shot."

She nodded and reached for the buttons on her blouse. She stepped out into the corridor and walked toward the guard, a forced smile on her face.

When she paused a few feet away from him, the Serb got to his feet and moved toward her, his weapon up and ready. Bolan stroked the trigger and the silenced pistol spit flame. A red hole appeared in the guard's temple, followed by a gout of dark red blood as the hollowpoint slug mushroomed in his brain. Petrova caught him as he fell and eased him to the floor.

The infirmary door wasn't locked so Bolan slipped in, followed by Petrova. In the dim light of the open door, he saw Kubura sleeping on one of the cots. Bolan leaned over the sleeping man and put his hand over his mouth.

"Dr. Kubura," he whispered into his ear, "I've come to get you out of here."

Kubura's eyes flashed open, and he struggled for a second before he recognized Bolan.

"Keep quiet," Bolan said as he took his hand away from the doctor's mouth, "and get dressed fast."

It took Kubura only a few seconds to pull on his clothes and grab his medical bag. "How did you get back here so fast?"

"Later," Bolan said.

The big American went back to the partially opened door and checked the corridor. Seeing that it was clear, he motioned for the two to follow him.

"Where are we going?" the doctor whispered.

"I have a vehicle at the bottom of the hill. We'll be back in Sarajevo before the sun comes up."

Bolan knew that the obvious escape route would be for them to take the twisting mountain road back down to where he had left the jeep. The problem was that most of the road was visible from the fortress, and there was no place to take cover if they were fired on. It would take longer for them to work their way down through the woods to the jeep, but it would be safer.

Keeping to the shadows of the wall, Bolan led the way toward the main gate. He had noticed a small door cut into the left-hand side of the main door. If they could get out that way, he wouldn't have to worry about Petrova and Kubura jumping down from the wall and injuring themselves.

"What do you think you are doing?" a voice called out from behind them. "That door is not to be opened after dark."

As Bolan spun to face the new threat, the doctor stepped out from behind him and walked toward the guard. "He said that I could go out whenever I wanted."

"Get back!" the Serb ordered. As he snapped down his AK-47 to fire, Bolan sidestepped, brought up his silenced pistol and triggered two quick rounds. Both of the light rounds connected, but didn't cause instant death. Reflexively the guard's finger tightened on the trigger, and the weapon fired a short burst.

Bolan snatched one of the grenades from his harness. Pulling the pin, he hurled the bomb through the air toward the pile of diesel fuel cans stacked beside the generator. The resulting explosion detonated several of the cans with a roar. Stepping over the guard's body, Bolan unlocked the side door and swung it open. "Let's go!" he yelled to Petrova and Kubura.

BOLAN LED THE WAY around the fortress to the east. By now, the guards were alert and firing their weapons into the darkness, but most of the gunfire from the battlements wasn't getting close to them. At the northeast corner of the wall, they made their break for the woods.

They were still twenty yards from the tree line when Bolan heard the distinctive whoosh of an RPG round leaving its launcher. "Get down!" he shouted.

The rocket detonated a few yards behind them. Since the RPG rocket was an antitank round, it didn't produce the same kind of deadly, man-killing shrapnel that a mortar round would have. Nonetheless, when the warhead detonated, the sheet steel of the rocket's outer skin fragmented into dozens of red-hot, razor-sharp chunks.

One of those thin chunks slammed into the back of Bolan's thigh, tearing into the muscle.

"Let's keep going," he said, gritting his teeth as he got to his feet.

He grabbed Kubura's shoulder for support as they hurried along the trail.

ZHINKOVITCH STRODE across the courtyard of the fortress, his eyes glittering in the flames of the fires that hadn't yet been put out. "I want that man," he growled at his troops. "I want the doctor and I want that woman. Find them and bring them back to me.''

That someone had had the audacity to come into his castle and steal the doctor and the woman from under his nose wasn't something that the warlord took lightly. He was Dushan Zhinkovitch, and his destiny was to rule. If he allowed that man to get away with this, he risked losing control over his people. He needed to make an example of the American, otherwise someone might get the idea that he could be bested and that wouldn't do. He was a man of the mountains, and he ruled because there was no one strong enough to oppose him.

By the time he'd reached puberty, Zhinkovitch had been as tall and as strong as most grown men. He had learned to use his strength to his advantage. He had gathered a small following who specialized in petty crime. Under Zhinkovitch's leadership, the gang soon graduated into bigger and more profitable criminal enterprises: smuggling, kidnapping and extortion.

Zhinkovitch and his gang continued their crime spree until the old Yugoslavian Republic broke up and he converted his band of smugglers and thieves into an armed militia. In the confusion of the time, arms and ammunition hadn't been difficult to come by. Deserters from the various national and factional armies also joined him, and he soon had a sizable fighting force.

Once his men were well armed, he started looking for a place to build his empire. At first, Zhinkovitch tried to carve out a holding on the plains, but the mechanized armies of the two new republics soon drove him back into the mountains. His men were tough, but they hadn't fared well against the heavy weaponry of regular troops.

After he was driven out of the plains, he had chanced on the fortress and settled in. Subduing and claiming the surrounding area had been merely a matter of showing the villagers that it was more to their advantage to live under his rule than to die under it. He now ruled a large enough area that his men had started calling him *ban,* the ancient Serbo-Croatian term for a duke. He liked the way it sounded, but was waiting until he could claim the name of king.

"Lazar is on the radio, Chief," Zhinkovitch's radioman announced, holding out the handset.

"We hit one of them," Lazar reported. "We found a trail of blood."

"Follow it and bring them back!" he roared.

In a few minutes, three tracking parties of experienced mountaineers were on the track of the fugitives, and Zhinkovitch was confident that they would be successful. There was no way that they could outrun his men on their home ground.

"Four of the guards are dead, sir," one of his troops told him.

"Dump their bodies over the wall," the warlord ordered. "If I catch anyone else sleeping on guard, he will go over the wall after them."

"Yes, Chief."

6

Even though he was wounded, Bolan took the lead as they fled into the mountains east of the warlord's fortress. He realized that trying to make it to Sarajevo would be suicide. Even with the jeep, once they were back down on the open plains, it would be too easy for Zhinkovitch's men to run them to ground. Their only hope was to try to lose their pursuers in the mountains.

After an hour Bolan called a rest break.

"Let me check your wound," Kubura said, opening his medical bag.

Bolan sat back against a tree while Kubura cut through the leg of his combat suit and probed the wound.

"It's not serious," the doctor said, "but I need to get that fragment out as soon as possible."

"Can you do it here?" Bolan asked.

Kubura shook his head. "I would try it if the wound was life-threatening, but there's too great a chance of it getting seriously infected. And with no light, I could cause even more damage while I'm poking around in there. I need light, boiled water and a clean place to work on you if you don't want to lose that leg."

"The way I see it, we don't have that many options right now," Bolan said. "If we go down into one of the villages, there's the risk that one of Zhinkovitch's men or a spy will be there and report us. Our only chance is to keep going until we lose them. How long can I go with that shrapnel in me?"

"There might be a way out," Kubura said thoughtfully.

"What's that?"

"There's a village not too far from here where we could stay while you recover."

"Won't it be in Zhinkovitch's area of influence?" Petrova asked. "He claims to control this whole region."

"No." The doctor shook his head. "It's in a hidden valley in the wild country to the east, and it's not accessible to motor vehicles. As far as I know, he's never been up there."

"How do you know about this place?" Bolan asked.

"One of my patients was from there," Kubura said, fighting to keep his voice under control as he thought of the young girl Zhinkovitch had killed.

"She'd left her village to visit a relative and was caught by Zhinkovitch's troops on one of their raids. Before she died, she told me about her village and how to get to it. There are a couple hundred refugees there. We'll be safe in the village until you're fit to travel again."

"How far is it?"

"She told me that it's a day's journey from the fortress."

Bolan looked at Petrova.

"It makes sense to me," she said. "I do not know this part of the country very well, but I do know that there are quite a few villages up here that are almost autonomous. No matter who thinks they control these mountains, the people live almost completely independent of government interference, as they have done for centuries."

"Okay," Bolan said. "We'll try it. Strap up my leg, Kubura, and let's get going."

After wrapping Bolan's thigh in a clean bandage, Kubura helped him to his feet, but Bolan waved off his offer of a shoulder for support. "I can walk," he said taking the point again.

A few miles on, the Executioner reached into his pouch and took out his compass. "Do you know how to use one of these?'' he asked Kubura.

The doctor nodded. "Back when I was in school, I did a little mountaineering."

"We've been moving almost due east," Bolan said, "and we've come about four miles. So head out the way you were told, but keep track of where we're going."

Kubura oriented himself with the compass. With him leading, the three made their way to the east.

ZHINKOVITCH LISTENED intently as he bent over the radio receiver in the command center of his fortress. "Are you certain that it is them?" he asked his lead tracker.

"I am certain, Chief," the voice on the other end said. "We found three sets of footprints. They are heading up into the mountains to the east instead of going down to the valley."

A slow smile crossed the warlord's face. The American was smarter than he had thought. He had expected him to head straight for the valley, like the city people always did. At least he'd had sense enough to stay in the mountains where there were more places to hide. But that wouldn't work either. Zhinkovitch was a man of the mountains, and no one would escape him on his home ground.

"Lazar," Zhinkovitch called out to his second in command, "put half a dozen horses into the trucks and get ready to drive up into the mountains. I know where the doctor has gone, and we are going to bring him back. I will take care of the American myself. But when we catch the woman, she will go into the barracks for all of you to enjoy."

A cheer broke out at that announcement. One of the reasons that Zhinkovitch's men were so loyal to him was that the warlord was generous with his booty. Women, gold or liquor—he shared it all, and no man could ask for more from a chief.

Zhinkovitch walked out into the courtyard. This was one manhunt he would lead himself.

KUBURA STOPPED at the top of the narrow, almost completely hidden trail. The midmorning sun had burned away the mist, and the valley below was bathed in full sunlight. They had kept on the move all night, with only short rest stops every hour. With Bolan's wounded leg, it had been somewhat slow going, but he had insisted that they keep on the march regardless. When the sun had come up, Kubura had recognized a landmark the girl had told him about, and he had guided them toward it.

"There it is," he said, pointing down the mountainside. "The village of Valliskya."

Bolan saw a large village in the center of a valley at least a mile and a half long by half a mile wide. Several dozen houses were clustered around a larger building in front of an open square. From what he could see, little brick or concrete had been used in any of the buildings. They all looked to be of the age-old stone and stucco construction of the region, which backed up the doctor's statement that the village had had little contact with the outside world.

It was easy to see how the place had remained cut off from the world for so long. Nestling in the small valley and surrounded by rugged mountains, the trail was more suited to goats than to humans. It wasn't impassable, but there was no way that a motor vehicle was going to get into it. No way at all. From what Bolan had seen of Zhinkovitch's troops, they weren't likely to have found it.

"It looks good to me," Bolan said. Like it or not, he knew that he had to have his leg seen to.

THEY WERE a hundred yards from the village when they saw a small delegation of men coming to meet them.

A man in his late sixties stepped forward and began to speak.

"He says that his name is Vlady Adan," Petrova translated. "He says that everyone is welcome here who leaves the hatred of the war behind."

Kubura stepped forward. "I am Dr. Kubura," he said in the Serbian dialect of Serbo-Croatian. "I treated one of your people, a teenaged girl, who had fallen into Dushan Zhinkovitch's hands. She spoke of your village and told me how to get here before she died."

"Who was this girl?" Adan asked.

"She said her name was Pavia."

A look of pain flashed across the old man's face. "She is dead?"

"Yes, I am sorry."

"You were held captive by Dushan Zhinkovitch?" Adan asked.

"The woman and I were," Kubura answered. "This man," he said, pointing to Bolan, "rescued us from him. He has been wounded, and I need a place to operate on him."

Adan looked at Bolan's combat suit, assault harness and weapons. He was obviously a soldier, but if what the doctor said was true, he was a soldier who was working to help people, not to hurt them. "You are welcome to stay with us until your friend is well enough to travel again."

"We have permission to stay," Kubura explained to Bolan.

Adan spoke to two of his men. "Take them to my house. The doctor can see to the soldier there."

WHEN BOLAN WOKE, he was lying on a narrow bed in a small room. The light told him that it was dusk, so he had been out most of the day. Turning his head, he saw a small boy sitting on a chair in the corner of the room.

"Where is the doctor?" Bolan asked in English.

Without saying a word, the boy got up and ran out of the room. A moment later, Kubura walked in. "How do you feel?" he asked.

"Okay," Bolan said. "Did you get it out?"

Kubura nodded. "I got the shrapnel out, cleaned the wound as well as I could and gave you a shot of antibiotics. You were lucky. As I thought, the fragment cut the muscles lengthwise rather than across. But all that walking with it in your leg didn't help it any. If you give that leg a rest for a while, though, it should heal with no problems.''

"How long will that take?'' Bolan asked. He was under no illusions about how safe they were, and he wanted them to be on their way as soon as possible. He didn't need to have a psych profile on Dushan Zhinkovitch to know that the Serb warlord probably had his men rooting under every bush in the mountains looking for them. They wouldn't be safe until they were back in Sarajevo, and he had put Kubura on a plane to the States.

"You lost quite a lot of blood, and you should keep off the leg for a couple of days."

"I don't think we're going to have that much time," Bolan said. "Find me something I can use for a crutch."

"As your doctor, I don't advise you to do that. You should rest."

"We don't have a choice," Bolan stated bluntly. "I have to be mobile."

Kubura sighed. "I'll see what I can find."

"Thanks."

As soon as Kubura had left, Petrova entered the room with Vlady Adan. "He wants to see how you are," she said, nodding toward the village chief.

"The doctor says I'm fine," Bolan replied. "All I need to do is rest for a couple of days. Ask him if Zhinkovitch knows about this place."

Adan shook his head when Petrova translated the question. "He says that the warlord's men have never been here. They go only to the villages they can get to in their trucks."

Bolan was glad to have his assessment confirmed, but he still didn't want to have to stay any longer than was absolutely necessary.

"Tell him that we'll be moving on as soon as we can."

7

Now that he had a crutch, Bolan was able to get around, although with some difficulty. He knew from long experience, though, that the healing process would be hastened with a little exercise. Plus, even though Kubura kept insisting that they were safe in Valliskya, he knew that they weren't. Zhinkovitch might be a throwback to the nineteenth-century bandit kings, but he was no fool. He was sure to have enough men who had been born and raised in these mountains to put together a good tracking team. The sooner they moved on, the better it would be for everyone concerned. The last thing he wanted to do was bring Zhinkovitch down on these people.

The villagers he passed on his walk greeted him. The differences between Serbs, Croatians or Muslims didn't seem to matter to them, as opposed to the ethnic war that was being fought just a few miles away.

ONE OF THE VILLAGERS watching Bolan walk past didn't greet him. Petar Simovitch was a Serb. The other villagers didn't know that he had served in the Serbian army, nor that he had deserted to avoid being court-martialed for stealing supplies. After leaving his regiment, he had stumbled upon the village and had been taken in like the rest of the refugees.

Life in the village hadn't been what Simovitch would have called comfortable. He had been put to work herding sheep, but he ate well and had put off moving on. Now, though, the three strangers had given him a good reason to leave. He had heard enough of the talk in the village to know that they were on the run from Dushan Zhinkovitch, the warlord who ruled almost everything in the region, except this hidden village.

Simovitch had briefly considered joining up with Zhinkovitch, but he was basically lazy and didn't really want to be in anyone's army again. However, it might be worth money to the man who led the warlord to the fugitives. And money was all Simovitch needed to get to one of the bigger cities and establish himself in the flourishing wartime black market.

It would be no trouble for him to slip away when he went out to tend the sheep in the morning. No one would miss him until evening and, even then, they probably wouldn't notice that he was gone. He had nothing of value to leave behind, but he knew that would change as soon as he reached the warlord with his news.

DUSHAN ZHINKOVITCH wasn't happy. The trackers had lost the trail of the three fugitives when they traversed a rocky area and had been stumbling around in the mountains for the past two days like blind men. They had searched every village and barn they had come across, but there was no sign of them. He hated to admit it, but it looked like they had somehow managed to escape the dragnet he had set out.

He was getting ready to return to the fortress when one of his scouts came up to him. "We picked up a man who says he wants to speak to you, Chief."

"Who is he?"

"He says that he is from a village around here, but I do not recognize the name. He says that he has information for you alone."

"Bring him."

The scout signaled, and two of his teammates walked into the clearing, escorting a civilian. When the man approached, he bowed his head respectfully.

"Who are you?"

"I am Petar Simovitch, sir," the man said. "I live in the village of Valliskya."

"What is that to me, you fool?" Zhinkovitch said. "All you stupid peasants live somewhere."

"I think that you are looking for two men and a woman," the man replied. "Strangers."

The Serb's eyes narrowed. "Where are they?"

"I think that this kind of information should be worth a reward."

Zhinkovitch glared at him. "That depends on who these people are."

"One of the men is an American doctor. The woman is Russian. The other man is a soldier and I think he is an American, too. They arrived two days ago and are hiding in my village until the soldier recovers from a wound." Simovitch shrugged. "I am a poor man. I want only enough money to get out of these mountains."

"I will see that you are rewarded," the warlord said. "You have the promise of Dushan Zhinkovitch. Tell me what you know."

"The people you are looking for are in the village of Valliskya," Simovitch said. "It is a half day's journey to the east and south from here, in a valley. If you head straight for it, you cannot miss it."

"Shoot him," Zhinkovitch coldly ordered one of his men.

"But you promised to reward me!" Simovitch cried.

"If you had brought me this news as a gift, you would have been rewarded because I am a generous man. But you came here to blackmail me, to force money from me like a thief, and for that you will die," Zhinkovitch responded.

"But you need me to lead you to this village. If it was an easy place to find, your men would have already come across it."

Zhinkovitch smiled. He liked a man who was sharp enough to know when he was holding the high card, and who had the balls to play it when the going got tough. Maybe there was more to this peasant than met the eye.

"You have a point, Simovitch. Like I said, I am a generous man. As the reward for your leading me to this village, I will forgive you for trying to blackmail me."

"You will not regret it," Simovitch said bowing his head again.

"I never regret anything that I do."

"THERE IT IS," Simovitch told Zhinkovitch, pointing to the valley spread out in front of them. "The village of Valliskya. The three people you are searching for are down there."

Zhinkovitch looked down into the valley. Because of the village's secluded position, his men had completely missed it when they had incorporated the surrounding area into his domain. That wouldn't last long, however. As soon as he could free more troops from his northern sector, he would garrison the valley and bring the villagers into his system.

For now, though, it would be enough to get the doctor back and to get his hands on the soldier. Zhinkovitch had sent a radio call to Sarajevo after the night attack on his fortress, but he had learned that they didn't know who the American was, either. They had told him that it wouldn't be a good idea for him to be killed, as his death could involve investigators who would look into their black market activities.

As far as Zhinkovitch was concerned, though, the Sarajevo mob was overly concerned about angering the United States and having the American aid supplies cut off. He understood their concern—much of their income was derived from misplaced American aid supplies. But he wanted that man, and he would have him. If they didn't like it, he would tell them to do their own dirty work the next time someone poked his nose into their network.

Studying the village through a powerful pair of field glasses, he couldn't see any signs of defenses. Whoever these people were, they were fools if they thought they could sit out the war hiding in their remote valley. Like all peasant farmers, all they thought about were their crops and animals. Zhinkovitch understood the minds of peasants. They were sheep who could be exploited by anyone strong enough to do so. These sheep would be no different.

He had only five men with him, but that should be enough to do what he had come to do now. The rest of it could wait until later. These peasants weren't going anywhere. To be sure, they were a little smarter than the average peasants; they had managed to hide in their valley until now. But he was confident that they wouldn't be smart enough to run again before he took care of them.

"Blas," he said to the squad leader, "take the point and get us down there without them seeing us."

"At once, Chief," the gunman said.

BOLAN WAS in the village chief's house when he heard the shot. He grabbed his AKM and, leaving the crutch behind, limped for the door. Looking out, he saw that there was some kind of commotion at the far end of the village.

When he arrived at the scene, he saw five men on horseback, with a riderless sixth horse standing by. The man on the lead horse was Dushan Zhinkovitch. Nina Petrova had her AK-47 centered on his chest, her finger on the trigger. One of the warlord's men lay on the ground by the spare horse, writhing in pain. Kubura was kneeling beside him, inspecting his wound.

Even though his men had their weapons trained on Petrova now, with the muzzle of her AK-47 locked on his heart, Zhinkovitch was careful not to make any sudden moves. He liked his women with a little fight in them, but he knew better than to trust a woman with a gun in her hands.

"Soldier," Zhinkovitch called out when he saw Bolan, "tell this woman to lower her weapon. I have come to talk."

"Not a chance," Bolan said as he brought his own AKM into a firing position. "You tell your men to throw down their guns and then we'll talk."

The warlord barked a command, and four AK-47s were slowly lowered to the ground.

"So talk," Bolan said.

"Why did you come to my home and take the doctor and the woman away from me?"

"Like I told you back there," Bolan said. "My President sent me to take Kubura back home, and I always do my job."

"You violated my hospitality."

Bolan stepped closer, his hand around the pistol grip of the assault rifle and his thumb on the selector switch. His gut instinct was to simply blast the Serb and his riders out of their saddles and be done with it. However, he knew that it would be better for the villagers if they could settle it without bloodshed.

"You certainly didn't treat me with any hospitality when you kidnapped the woman and ran me out of your castle," Bolan said. "We came in peace under the protection of the UN, but you didn't respect that."

"I want the doctor, and I intend to have him. If I have to tear down this place to get him, I will," Zhinkovitch said.

"I don't want to see a war here," Bolan said. "These people took us in only because I was hurt. They aren't part of your argument with me."

By now, Kubura had patched up the wounded Serb. The man got back on his horse.

"Doctor," the warlord said, "I want you to leave this place and come back with me."

Kubura shook his head. "No. I have to go back to Sarajevo. I have done everything I can for your son, and it is time that I got back to my work at the hospital."

"I will be back, soldier," the warlord warned Bolan. "Next time, I will bring all my men. There is no way that you can stand against me."

The warlord jerked his horse's head around and galloped toward the hills.

"I am afraid that we have not seen the last of him," Petrova said as she watched the Serbs start back up the trail.

Bolan could only nod in agreement.

8

Petrova kept her AK-47 at the ready until the Serbs were completely out of sight. Only then did she sling the assault rifle. "I should have killed the bastard while I had the chance," she said.

Bolan knew that while that would have solved one immediate problem, it could well have created several others. This way, there was still a chance that Zhinkovitch would rethink his threat to return or at least give Bolan enough time to prepare for his next visit. What had started out as a simple mission gone bad had just taken a more serious turn. And, with his injured leg, his options weren't as good as he would have liked.

Bolan took the village chief aside to talk to him. Their safe haven was now in danger of becoming a battlefield, which was the last thing the Executioner wanted.

"Do your people have any weapons?" he asked through Petrova.

"Some of us have rifles and shotguns for hunting," Adan said, "but we do not fight wars."

"I understand that you want to live in peace here," Bolan said, "but I think that your people are going to have to fight this time, or you're all going to die. Zhinkovitch was serious when he said that he'll come back with his army. It would be a good idea for your people to be ready for him."

Adan slowly shook his head. "We came here to get away from the fighting, not to fight even more. My people are not soldiers, they are just farmers and herdsmen. All they want to do is to live simply and in peace."

"That may not be possible now. Zhinkovitch knows about your village, and also that you have taken us in," Bolan pointed out.

"We will hide you if Zhinkovitch comes back," Adan said firmly, "but we will not fight him."

"If you won't fight," Bolan said, "my friends and I have to leave here immediately. But I'm afraid that won't save you either. Now that Zhinkovitch knows of your existence, he won't rest until you are under his control. Unless you want to become his slaves, you'll have to fight. You don't really have any other choice."

The chief thought for a moment. "I will discuss what you have said with the village council," he finally said. "But I must tell you that I will vote for peace myself."

"That will be a vote for slavery," Bolan said, "not peace. You can't have peace when another man's boot is on your neck."

When Adan didn't answer him, Bolan pressed the point. "Can I talk to the council myself? If they decide to fight, I'll stay here to help organize your men. If they decide not to fight, we'll leave immediately so as not to make things any worse for you."

The chief nodded his consent. "We have been cut off from the outside world for a long time. Maybe we need to hear the words of an outsider."

"HEY, SOLDIER!" The small, dark-haired man with jet black eyes called out in English as Bolan limped past him.

Bolan turned. "Are you talking to me?"

The man laughed. "Of course I am talking to you. How many other soldiers have you seen in this place?"

"How do you know that I'm a soldier?"

"I am a Gypsy," he said. "I know these things. I also know that you are going to have a big problem if you try to get these people to defend themselves."

"Why is that?"

"Most of these people went through hell before they ended up here. All they want to do is live peacefully. But you and I both know that peace is something that a man has to make for himself."

Bolan smiled. "What is a philosopher doing here?"

The Gypsy shrugged. "Everyone has to be somewhere, soldier. But now that you are here, maybe I can be somewhere else. I would like to go with you when you leave."

"What makes you think that I'm going anywhere?"

"You do not look like a crazy man to me," the Gypsy said, "so why would you want to stay here?"

When Bolan didn't answer immediately, the man stepped closer to him. "I see that I was wrong about you. You are not just a soldier, you are a warrior and that is not good."

The Gypsy shook his head. "Warriors always want to right all the wrongs of the world. They always stand and fight when a man of good sense would turn and run. They are very dangerous to a man like me who wants only to live his life in peace. When there is a warrior around, trouble is never far behind him."

"If you are looking for peace," Bolan said, "you're in the wrong place. Now that Zhinkovitch knows of this village, peace is going to be hard to come by around here."

"Maybe it will be more peaceful if you and the Russian woman leave."

"That won't stop Zhinkovitch from taking it out on these people for having sheltered us. Nor will it prevent him from trying to take control of this place."

"I am afraid that you are right," the Gypsy admitted. "If you take me with you, I will not be here to suffer with them."

"What is your name?"

The small man shrugged. "My name is not important," he said. "They just call me Gypsy because I am the only one of my kind here."

"Okay, Gypsy, I'll think about taking you with us when we go."

"I know a secret," the man said.

"Is this another Gypsy thing?"

"No. This secret is something that even a dumb Serb would know if he went to the right place. I know where there is a supply of Russian weapons and ammunition close by."

"Where?" Now the man had Bolan's complete attention. Even if he left, if he could change Adan's mind about self-defense, the arms could be put to good use. "How did they get there?"

"When the Russians left Yugoslavia, one of their battalion commanders had his men take some of their weapons and ammunition to a place where he was going to sell them to the Serbs. The Serb contact had an 'accident,' however, and could not make it to the meeting place to pay for them. The Russian commander left them there hoping that he could find another buyer. He, too, had an 'accident' before he could do that, so they are still there."

"I take it that you had a hand in those accidents?"

"Maybe." The Gypsy shrugged. "The only thing that is important is that I know where those weapons are."

"Will you show me where they are?"

"Do you intend to arm these farmers and teach them how to fight?"

Bolan nodded.

"All right," the man said. "If you will promise to take me out of here if we both survive, I will show you where the guns are."

"It's a deal."

BOLAN FOUND Kubura in the makeshift infirmary he had set up, attending to a young girl.

"You know that Zhinkovitch is going to come back here looking for you," Bolan said.

"I know," Kubura said. "I've been thinking about that. I've decided that I'm not going back to Sarajevo with you. I'm going to stay here because these people need me more than the people do in the city. I can do more good here, and there are other doctors in Sarajevo."

"As you well know, my mission has nothing to do with these villagers," Bolan said. "The President sent me to rescue you and take you back to the United States."

He raised his hand to forestall the doctor's reply. "If you don't want to go back with me, I can't force you, but I can stay here with you and try to change your mind. But if you want to really help these people, come with me now so there'll be no reason for Zhinkovitch to attack them."

"I can't do that," Kubura said. "They need me here. I know Zhinkovitch won't kill me when he comes back. I operated on his son, and he wants me to continue to be his private doctor. I think that I can make a bargain with him where he'll allow me to help these people if I agree to treat his troops."

"You haven't much to bargain with," Bolan pointed out. "The last time you tried to save a civilian, he killed her.

"Zhinkovitch will have no problem with these villagers. He wants to incorporate this place into his growing empire, and if these people are of no use to him, he'll kill them, just like he killed the girl at his fortress."

"The girl was killed to punish me," the doctor said. "So I would not 'waste my time on her' as he put it."

"I don't know if you really understand what kind of person you're dealing with here," Bolan said. "You can't bargain with a man like Zhinkovitch, because he answers to no one. He's a law unto himself, a dictator with no one to keep him from doing anything he wants to do. No matter what you say, or what he agrees to, he'll do whatever he wants."

"I still have to try," Kubura insisted. "I came to this country to help the victims of the war. They need my help more than they do in Sarajevo, or in the States."

"If you're going to stay here and try to save these people your way, then I'm going to have to try to help them my way. I've been told of a nearby cache of Russian weapons, and I'm going to try to arm these people so they can defend themselves. It's the only thing I can do to help them from being slaughtered like animals."

"I don't think you'll get them to fight," Kubura said. "They came here to escape the war."

"I'm afraid that the fight has come to them, whether they want it or not," Bolan stated. "I'm going to talk to the village council tonight. It'll be their call."

Kubura had no answer to that.

THAT NIGHT, Vlady Adan and the village council met in the chief's house to discuss Bolan's proposal to arm themselves and fight Zhinkovitch if he came back. The majority of the men wanted to fight to protect what was theirs. Now that the warlord knew of their existence, they realized the danger they were in.

When Bolan told them of the weapons cache the Gypsy had told him about, they voted overwhelmingly to defend themselves.

"I hope you're happy," Kubura said as they left the meeting. "These people are getting themselves into something that's going to turn their lives upside down. Nothing good is going to come from this."

"I'm not happy about any of this," Bolan replied. "But you heard what they said in there.

They want to start defending themselves, so if I can help them in any way, I'll do it.''

"Don't expect me to applaud what you're doing."

Bolan looked him square in the eye. "I don't," he said. "But at the same time, don't expect me to stand here and let these people get slaughtered."

9

Early the next morning, Bolan had the Gypsy round up six of the village's horses so he could investigate the weapons cache before he took the plan any further.

"If we're not back by nightfall," Bolan told Petrova as they were leaving, "it means we've run into trouble, so don't bother sticking around. Take off and try to make it back to Sarajevo. I don't think that Kubura will come with you, so don't worry about him. Just get yourself out."

"Be careful."

Bolan patted the buttstock of his AKM. "I will."

A slow two-hour ride into the mountains brought them to a limestone cave in a ravine. Thick brush had grown up over the entrance, and it looked as if no one had been there for years.

"How did they find this place?" Bolan asked as he slid off his horse.

The Gypsy pointed down the ravine to the south. "There is a road from here that leads down to a main highway. There was a Russian army camp twelve kilometers away. This was a safe, out-of-the-way place, but they could still get their trucks up here."

Pulling the brush aside, the Gypsy went into the cave and came out dragging a wooden crate with Russian script stenciled on it. Bolan was able to translate to markings to see that the crate contained ten AK-47 assault rifles.

"There are five of these crates," the Gypsy said, "as well as some other weapons and ammunition for them."

Bolan followed him into the cave and was glad to see that the weapons cache was everything the man had said it was. The only way a confrontation with Zhinkovitch had even half a chance of turning out well, was for the villagers to get their hands on some modern military weapons.

Along with the fifty Kalashnikov assault rifles, there were at least five hundred rounds of 7.62 mm ammunition for each of them. Behind the crates were two RPG-7 antitank rocket launchers and two dozen rockets. An RPG was just as simple to use as an AK-47 and was foolproof as well as effective. There were also several dozen Russian RDG-5 style hand grenades and several thousand rounds of the 7.62 mm rimmed ammunition for the RP-46 series of machine guns, although the guns themselves weren't there. There would hopefully be several versions of the bolt-action Russian Mosin-Nagant rifle in the village, and the machine-gun ammunition could be stripped from the belts and used in the Russian rifles.

All told, it was as good a supply of weapons as anything Bolan could have had flown in from the States. Better, in some ways, because they were simpler to use and didn't need expert maintenance. He would have liked to have had a little more ammunition so he could spend more time teaching the villagers how to use the assault rifles effectively. But he could allot thirty rounds— one full magazine—to each man for familiarization and still have enough left over to fight with, as long as it didn't become a long, drawn-out assault.

"Let's get this stuff loaded up," Bolan said, reaching for one of the crates. "I want to get these AK-47s issued today and start showing the villagers how to use them."

After quickly loading the weapons and ammunition onto the four packhorses, they headed back for the village.

BOLAN FOUND a large reception committee waiting for them when he and the Gypsy returned. Apparently the members of the village council weren't the only ones who thought that it was time they learned how to defend themselves. Almost every male from nine to ninety was on hand to see what they had found.

After they had unloaded the weapons, the first dozen men were issued AK-47s for cleaning under the Gypsy's supervision. Since the assault rifles had been in long-term storage, they had been packed in the Russian equivalent of petroleum, and every last bit of the protective grease had to be cleaned off before they could be fired. There was a lack of chemical solvents in the village, but several quarts of lamp kerosene were found that would work almost as well.

Once that chore was underway, Bolan had Petrova put some of the village women to work loading the AK-47 magazines from the stripper clips the assault rifle ammunition came packed in. Another group of women stripped the 7.62 mm rimmed ammunition from the machine-gun belts for use in the Mosin-Nagant bolt-action rifles.

Bolan went through the collection of older weapons and ammunition the villagers had gathered for him to examine. Most of them were bolt-action rifles left over from World War II, but there were a few World War I vintage Mausers and Mosin-Nagants, as well as a single French 8 mm Lebel. There were also the odd German Luger and P-38 pistols, and a few Russian Tokarevs. For a supposedly peaceful farming village, these people were well armed. The problem with most of the older weapons, however, was that they hadn't been maintained.

Starting with the 7.62 mm Russian Mosin-Nagant rifles because he had more ammunition for them, Bolan started breaking the rifles down and inspecting them to see if they were still serviceable. Since the rifle had been in production for decades, it was a simple matter for him to change bolts to bring a rifle back into service.

When he was done, he had a dozen of the Russian bolt-action rifles that would stand up under sustained firing. One of them was a well-preserved Model 1891/30 left over from World War II with the iron sights graduated out to 2,400 yards. The rifling inside the long barrel was still bright, and it would make a good sniper's weapon. He laid aside that rifle for his own use.

Several of the World War II German and Yugoslav Mausers were still serviceable, but he had less than a hundred rounds of the 7.62 mm ammunition for them, and most of it was in questionable condition. With the AK-47s and the Mosin-Nagants he had on hand, he could reserve the Mausers for an emergency.

Bolan turned his attention to his defense strategies for the village. Since the valley was surrounded by hills, if Dushan Zhinkovitch was smart, he would simply take possession of the high ground and rain heavy-weapons fire on them until it was all over.

The Executioner suspected that the warlord wouldn't be content to do that, however. He'd want to come down and fight it out at close range. That was what Bolan hoped he would do. The villagers' only chance was to get Zhinkovitch's thugs down on the valley floor. A house-to-house fight was what was needed in order to win. They would be on the defensive, and they needed to dig in.

After showing the villagers where he wanted the first of the fighting positions dug, Bolan returned to the makeshift firing range to take over the firing instruction.

KUBURA FROWNED when he heard the distinctive clatter of an AK-47 firing on full-automatic. A few minutes later, one of the villagers walked past the infirmary with a rifle slung over his right shoulder and a bandoleer of ammunition maga-

zines slung over his left. Apparently they were
going to give up their long-held pacifism and
fight after all. The doctor felt angry. These people had survived the insanity that had swept
through the new Yugoslavian republics by not
getting involved, and now they were going to
throw it all away.

The doctor wasn't a coward, but after working in the Sarajevo hospital for so many months,
he had had enough of the war. As far as he was
concerned, anything that would bring the fighting to a halt was good. Arming the villagers
against Zhinkovitch was sheer idiocy. They were
farmers, not soldiers. If they had wanted to
fight, they wouldn't have come to Valliskya in the
first place. He knew that it wasn't their idea to
fight. Jordan—if that was his real name—had
promoted this madness and had infected them
with it.

He understood that the man's intentions were
well meant, but he also believed that they were
dead wrong and would only bring misery to the
villagers. He knew that there was no point in his
trying to talk the man out of his plan. He had
known men of action like him before, and the
last thing they listened to was reason.

Kubura knew that it would take action as well,
not talk, to stop Jordan and prevent a tragedy

from happening in this place. Now that the villagers had voted to follow the man, there was no one to take that action apart from himself. The Russian woman certainly wouldn't. He had seen the way she looked at Jordan, and he knew there would be no help coming from her. He had no idea of where to start, but he would think of something before Jordan brought the horror of the rest of the country to this island of sanity.

THAT EVENING, Bolan, Petrova and the Gypsy held a meeting. Even though all the AK-47s had been cleaned and the first dozen or so fighting positions dug, there was still a great deal to be planned.

Bolan turned to the small man. "In the morning, Adan has promised me a large work party to continue digging the fighting positions. I'd like you to oversee that."

"They listen to me well enough when I tell them how to clean their rifles," he replied, "but I do not think that they will follow my orders when I tell them to do something like that."

"Why not?" Bolan frowned.

"Because I am a Gypsy. For a long time now, my people have not been greatly appreciated around here."

"I thought that this was the one place in this country where people could put their differences aside and work for the common good."

"They can," the man replied. "Just as long as you don't try to include Gypsies."

"I'll talk to Adan about this first thing in the morning," Bolan said, "and explain to him that you are part of the leadership team here."

The man shrugged. "Try it and then maybe you will understand the situation better."

Bolan smiled. "I can be pretty convincing."

"If you were able to convince these people to defend themselves, you should be able to talk the devil himself out of hiding," the Gypsy admitted.

"Nina," Bolan said, turning to Petrova, "in the morning, I'm also going to start forming the men into squads. I'll need you to translate for me and help me figure out who to put in leadership positions."

"I'll talk to Adan and get his advice on who is reliable."

"Good idea."

"And what about the doctor?" she asked. "I do not think that he is behind you on this."

"He isn't," Bolan admitted. "Even though he saw the way Zhinkovitch operates, he still thinks that it's possible to come to some sort of arrangement with him.''

The Gypsy snorted. "If the doctor thinks that Dushan Zhinkovitch will be reasonable, he needs to take some of his own medicine because he is very sick.''

"There are a lot of Americans who don't think that men like Zhinkovitch exist,'' Bolan said.

"They should come and live here for a while. Maybe then they would learn otherwise.''

10

Dushan Zhinkovitch wasn't a man to fly into a rage unless that rage could accomplish something, but he was finding it difficult to keep his temper under control. Not only had he been run out of Valliskya the day before, but when he had returned to his fortress headquarters, he had a message telling him that a band of renegade Croats was raiding the villages in his northern territory. Normally an attack on what he regarded as his sovereignty would be swiftly crushed, but there was nothing he could do about it until he had finished his business with the village. He couldn't be at two places at the same time, and dealing with Valliskya came first.

He could afford to let renegade Croats get away with nipping at his northern border, but he couldn't allow any of the villagers in his realm to defy him. He knew that if those peasants humiliated him without being severely punished, the other villages under his control would think they could get away with doing the same thing.

With winter coming on, he had to secure his supplies or his army would suffer. His men followed him because he fed them well and saw that they had liquor and women to amuse themselves during the long winter months. All three of those commodities came from the villages under his control, and he had to keep that supply line open at all costs. That meant bringing Valliskya under control before word got out that the people had defied him.

If he left his heavy weapons at the fortress to defend it in his absence, he had sixty men he could spare for the operation against Valliskya. He figured that the villagers were armed—everyone had some kind of weapon nowadays. But their weapons would be left over from the old wars that had passed through the region, mostly old German or Russian bolt-action rifles. During his brief visit to the village, he had seen no defensive positions and nothing to indicate that they had machine guns or mortars. Sixty men with AK-47s and RPGs should be more than enough to completely wipe out the place.

Calling for his messenger, Zhinkovitch gave the orders to prepare to move out against Valliskya.

THE MORE KUBURA THOUGHT about Jordan handing out weapons and training the villagers in their use, the more he didn't like it. When he saw that the villagers were digging foxholes—or whatever they were called—in strategic positions, he knew the only result would be bloodshed. Zhinkovitch's men were seasoned fighters, and he knew that the warlord would show no mercy to anyone who defied him. His renegade troops would crush the villagers, and it was all Jordan's fault.

Kubura knew that he was supposed to be grateful to the man for having rescued him from Zhinkovitch. But there was something about the big man that left him cold. That Jordan was military, he had no doubt now. But whatever the man's true identity, Kubura was convinced that Jordan was a threat to both himself and to the villagers who had taken him in. It was true that back in the fortress Kubura would have gladly killed Zhinkovitch himself, but that blind, unthinking rage had passed. Now he was back to thinking like a doctor, and that meant preventing bloodshed at any cost. He'd have to somehow outsmart the big American.

Kubura knew that he couldn't win in a face-to-face confrontation with the big man, but perhaps if he betrayed him to the warlord . . .

Even though Kubura had no military training, he was sure that Zhinkovitch was having the
village watched. The warlord wanted him, and it
made sense that he'd be keeping a close eye on
the place. If he could somehow sneak out and
find the watchers, he could get word to the Serb
that Jordan was preparing a defense, and pro-
pose a way out of the situation without anyone
getting hurt. If Zhinkovitch agreed to his terms,
he could arrange to lead in the warlord and his
men so they could take over the village without
killing anyone.

It would be easy enough to do. He had a good
supply of a powdered barbiturate in his medical
bag. All he would have to do was to put some of
it in the coffee, and he could insure that not only
Bolan, but the Russian woman and the Gypsy
would be put to sleep, as well.

No one would be expecting it. It would also be
easy for him to get out of the village. Since everyone was busy with their new war toys, no one
would notice that he was even gone.

EVEN THOUGH there was so much to get ready,
Zhinkovitch had taken time to check in on his
son. The boy's leg was healing well, but he still
wanted the doctor back to make sure it continued that way. He had seen too many men crip-

pled from that kind of accident. His son couldn't take over his empire if he was crippled—the men wouldn't follow him.

He was leaving his son's room when the duty runner found him. "Lazar says that he has the American doctor on the radio and he wants to talk to you."

"About what?"

"He says that he has a proposition for you. A way to deliver the village to us."

Zhinkovitch smiled. This was unexpected, but it wasn't beyond the realm of possibility. He often had this effect on lesser men. Once they had been exposed to him and had seen the greatness of his dreams, they wanted to be a part of them. Maybe this would be a way for him to deal with the village and stop the raids on his northern border at the same time. If the doctor could deliver the village to him, then he wouldn't have to send the bulk of his forces there, but could use them against the Croats.

Another man might have thought that Kubura was setting a trap, but he knew better. The doctor didn't have it in him to do something that brave. The man was weak, and weak men didn't plan treachery against someone like himself. Kubura had simply come to his senses and realized that it made more sense for him to attach himself to a strong man.

"Doctor," Zhinkovitch said over the radio, "I understand that you want to cooperate with me."

"I want to save the villagers from bloodshed," Kubura answered. "The soldier is talking them into resisting you, and he had found a supply of weapons with which to arm them."

"What kind of weapons?"

"I don't know anything about guns, but they look like the same as the ones your men have."

That made the warlord pause. If the soldier had found a cache of AK-47s, it could create a problem. But if he could get in there fast enough, the peasants wouldn't have time to learn how to use them. "What is your proposal?" he asked.

"If you will give me your word that the villagers will not be harmed and that the soldier and the Russian woman will be released, I will make sure that your men get into the village without being spotted. Once they are inside, they will be able to disarm the guards."

"You have my word," the warlord readily agreed. "The villagers will not be harmed, and I will let the soldier and the woman go free. How soon can you do this?"

"Tonight, if you can get here."

"Where do I meet you?"

"On the east side of the village, about two hundred yards from the houses. There is a big hayrick there. You can't miss it. I will be there at two o'clock."

"Get two dozen men ready," Zhinkovitch ordered as he set down the radio handset. "We ride for Valliskya tonight."

KUBURA POURED HIMSELF a mug of coffee before carefully adding a measured amount of the powdered barbiturate to the rest of the pot. He needed to stay awake so he could lead Zhinkovitch's men in through the gaps in the perimeter Bolan had established around the village. After the pot was doctored, he put it back on the fire in the room Bolan and the Gypsy had been occupying. Petrova was eating with them as well, so she would also take her coffee from that pot.

He mixed Bolan's dose of barbiturates into a glass of water with a powdered antibiotic he had been giving him to insure his wound didn't become infected. "Here you are," he said, handing over the cup. "I don't want that wound becoming infected at this stage."

Since he had the early-morning guard shift, Bolan drained his cup, then lay on his bunk and immediately fell asleep.

ZHINKOVITCH WAITED in the darkness with half a dozen of his men spread around him. The rest of them waited five hundred yards away with the horses, ready to sweep in if there was any trouble.

It was a little before two o'clock when Kubura appeared. "Everything is ready," he said. "They are all asleep and will sleep until morning. I gave them a sleeping powder in their coffee."

"Where are these defenses?"

"So far, the soldier has dug only a few foxholes on the other side of the village, and most of the guards are on watch from their houses. I found a way in from the north. No one is watching that direction."

"You have done well, Doctor. I will not forget this."

"I didn't do this for me," Kubura said. "I just don't want to see any harm come to these people."

"I will take good care of them," Zhinkovitch said. "You can be sure of that."

ONCE THE WORD WAS GIVEN, the doctor was surprised to see how quickly the warlord's men sprang into action. Zhinkovitch kept him at his side and stayed back, while the troops silently breached the perimeter. The warlord had given orders that as many of the villagers were to be taken alive as possible, but regardless of any promises he had made to the doctor, the village was to be taken, one way or the other.

When it was light enough to see, Zhinkovitch moved on into the village himself and took Kubura with him. One of the first things the doctor saw was the body of one of the village men lying in the dirt with his throat cut.

"You promised me that no one would be harmed."

The warlord shrugged. "Only those who resisted were killed. Surely you did not think that I was going to allow these filthy peasants to kill my soldiers? This whole village and everyone in it is not worth the life of a single one of my men."

Kubura looked at Zhinkovitch in horror. He had gambled on the man's sense of honor, but he had none. His betrayal of Jordan had been for nothing.

BOLAN WOKE to someone roughly shaking him. Opening his heavy eyes, he saw the muzzles of several AK-47s aimed at him. Something was desperately wrong. Blinking to clear his vision, he looked past the assault rifles and saw the grinning faces of Serbs in camouflage uniforms.

He felt woozy and realized that he had been drugged. Someone had betrayed them to Zhinkovitch.

Hands grabbed him, and he was jerked to his feet. He was pushed against the wall and patted down for hardware. After he was found to be clean, he was prodded outside with the muzzles of their rifles.

When they reached the village square, Bolan saw that Petrova had also been captured. One side of her face was bruised, and her hands were bound behind her. Two armed gunmen stood on either side of her, the muzzles of their assault rifles pressed into her ribs. He didn't see the Gypsy, but he knew that he would survive. His kind always did.

The villagers were being gathered in the square as well. In the light of early dawn, Bolan saw more of Zhinkovitch's men moving from house to house, rousing the villagers and adding them to the catch. Several of the men bore bloody evidence that they hadn't come willingly. The women were holding their smaller children in their arms and sheltering the older ones behind them as the gunmen separated them from their husbands and fathers. So far, he hadn't seen any bodies.

Apparently the Serbs had somehow achieved complete surprise while he had been in a drugged sleep. Petrova and the Gypsy had obviously been drugged as well.

When Zhinkovitch stepped out into the square, Bolan saw Kubura walking beside him and instantly knew what had happened. In his desire to prevent bloodshed, the doctor had doomed the villagers to slavery, if not death.

Why hadn't the man agreed to go back to Sarajevo with Bolan when he'd had the chance? Or why hadn't he simply taken the doctor by force, regardless of what Kubura had wanted? Bolan realized it had been a dangerous lapse on his part, but it was too late now for him to do anything except play the cards he had been dealt.

11

Zhinkovitch signaled for his gunmen to release Bolan and motioned for him to come forward. He halted in front of the Serbian and waited for him to speak first. If this was to be the end of the road, he would face it head-on, as he had faced everything else that life had thrown his way. But he also knew that the road didn't end until the final step had been taken, and so far he was still on his feet.

The warlord stared at Bolan for a long moment before speaking. "At first I wanted to kill you for what you had done to me, soldier," he said. "But now, when I look at what you have led me to—" his arms swept out to encompass the surroundings "—I am willing to be generous.

"You have made it possible for me to bring all of this under my control. My men need to eat, and these people have done well with their crops.

So I am going to let you go unharmed. Leave here now and I will trouble you no more."

Bolan had seen too much in his life to be surprised at this unexpected turn of events and decided to press his luck while it was running his way. "What about the Russian woman and Dr. Kubura?"

"Those who know me say that I am a reasonable man as well as a generous one. Since the woman seems to be so important to you, she can go with you. Consider her a gift from me to you.

"The doctor, no. He agreed to stay here with me, so he must stay. I need him to take care of my men and their families. What kind of leader would I be if I did not care for my followers?"

Bolan looked at the doctor, but Kubura stared at the ground in front of him and wouldn't meet his eyes.

Zhinkovitch smiled. "Tell your President of the great generosity I have shown to you. Tell him that if he will send me a medical team like the ones he sends to the cities, I will give him the doctor in return. As I said, I am a reasonable man."

Bolan looked him straight in the eye. "You can be sure I will tell the President what you have said."

When Zhinkovitch motioned to the men guarding Petrova, they dropped their muzzles. She quickly walked to Bolan's side and stood close to him. Her face was pale.

"Are you okay?" he asked, keeping his voice low.

She nodded.

Two saddled horses were brought up, while four mounted Serbs waited alongside, their fingers on the triggers of their AK-47s.

They both mounted and turned the horses toward the trail leading to the west. Their escort pulled in behind them and followed them out. At the edge of the village, Bolan turned in his saddle and saw that Kubura was still standing beside the warlord. The doctor had made his bed, and now he would have to lie in it. He didn't think that Kubura was going to find it too comfortable, though.

At the top of the ridge line overlooking the valley, the leader of the escort pulled his horse to a halt and pointed down the trail through the mountains. Slowly looking Petrova up and down, he said something in Serbo-Croatian.

"He says that if we are seen here again," she translated, "you will be shot on sight. I will not tell you what he said would happen to me."

"Tell him that we are going," Bolan said, "and we won't return."

The man jerked the neck of his horse around. He was anxious to get back to the village before all the good-looking women were claimed. Spurring on his mount, he led the others away at a gallop.

"YOU CAN COME OUT now," Bolan said, as soon as the Serbian escort was out of sight.

There was a rustle in the brush on the side of the trail and out stepped the Gypsy. His knife was in his belt, and he had an AK-47 slung over his shoulder, as well as a full magazine pouch attached by a length of rope.

"I am glad that you made it out alive," he said. "I did not think that Zhinkovitch would let you go."

"What happened to you back there?" Bolan asked.

"I was walking around the perimeter checking on the men, when I suddenly became very tired. I sat down, and the next thing I knew it was morning and some Serb was kicking me. I managed to cut his throat and take his rifle. Then I saw that there were dozens of them, and that almost everyone had been taken prisoner."

"You managed to get away, though," Bolan said.

"I am good at what I do, soldier. Before I left, I also took care of that Serb Petar Simovitch, who first told Zhinkovitch where you were. He betrayed me, too, and it is unwise to betray a Gypsy. I cut his throat as a warning to the others, so now I can go with you."

"I know I promised that you could come with me," Bolan said, "but I'm going back to Valliskya, not to Sarajevo."

The small man looked over at Petrova. "I suppose that you are going to take her with you. That is what a warrior does. He enlists other fools to his banner and takes them to their deaths as well."

He spit on the ground. "You are both fools."

Bolan looked at the man. "What do you want me to do, run to safety and leave those people to Zhinkovitch and his thugs?"

"Why not?" the small man shot back. "Some people are not willing to pay the price to live free. They fled their original homes because they would not fight, so why should they fight now?"

"Sometimes it takes as much courage to run as it does to fight. You should know that."

The Gypsy's hand went to his knife hilt, but he didn't draw it. The big man was right. His people had survived as long as they had only because they had known when to run and when to fight. There were no heroic, but futile, last stands in the history of the Gypsy's people. When things got too rough, they simply packed their wagons and left.

"Do you have a plan?" the man asked.

"The way I figure it," Bolan said, "Zhinkovitch's men will probably celebrate their victory tonight. There'll be a lot to drink, so a couple of men with knives should be able to cut the odds down quite a bit before the shooting starts."

The Gypsy was silent for a long moment. "You are going back to Valliskya where there are two dozen Serbs, and you are going to risk your life to free those who would not fight to free themselves." He shook his head.

"That's one way of looking at it," Bolan said. "But, remember, they decided that they wanted to fight, and I promised them that I would teach them what they need to know."

"So, what do we do next?" the Gypsy asked.

"We wait until dark."

ZHINKOVITCH DIDN'T stay around long after the soldier and the woman had ridden away. Now that the village had been secured, he needed to turn his attention to dealing with the Croats raiding his northern boundary. Lazar, his second in command, would take care of what had to be done in Valliskya.

"Do not be too hard on them," he told Lazar. "We need them to produce for us. But, at the same time, I do not want them to think that they can ever defy me again."

"Do not worry, Chief," Lazar said smiling. "They will never forget what it means to cross Dushan Zhinkovitch."

As the warlord rode off with his escort, half of the troops he had left behind guarded their prisoners, while the other half began to search the village for loot. Only after any valuables had been secured would they start in on the village's women and alcohol.

KUBURA WAS STARTLED to hear a scream from one of the women. Looking up, he saw one of the Serbs grappling with a young woman. "Leave her alone," he shouted.

When the Serb ignored him, Kubura ran to find the man Zhinkovitch had left in charge of his troops. Lazar was in the village tavern he had taken over as his command post. "What is it?" he asked impatiently when Kubura burst in the door.

"One of your men is molesting a woman."

"Just molesting her, you say." Lazar chuckled. "She is a lucky one, then."

"Your leader promised me that the villagers would not be harmed," Kubura protested. "Please tell your men to leave them alone."

"You fool," Lazar said. "Did you think he was going to let these pigs think that they had gotten away with defying him? They are going to be taught a lesson that their grandchildren will remember."

"But why? He has what he wants. The soldier is gone and all the guns have been collected. These people are not resisting him anymore, so why can't he leave them in peace?"

Lazar shook his head in mock dismay. "I do not know what the chief sees in you. You are the biggest fool I have ever known. These people rebelled against their master, and they must be taught never to think of doing that again. As you yourself have seen, the chief is not a man to be crossed."

"I won't let you do this," Kubura shouted.

The doctor never saw the rifle butt that Lazar slammed into his stomach.

"Get him out of here," the Serb called to one of his troops. "Take him to wherever he is staying and keep him there."

Retching and gagging, Kubura didn't resist as he was taken away.

BOLAN, PETROVA AND the Gypsy spent the day keeping watch on the village. As the Executioner had expected, an overly confident Zhinkovitch had pulled in all of his outposts now that he thought Bolan was gone and the village was under his control. Plus, he knew that the Serb had let his men enjoy the spoils of Valliskya without delay.

The people of Valliskya would pay a heavy price this day, but there was nothing Bolan could do about that. His only hope was that Zhinkovitch's troops would leave enough of the men alive that he could reconstitute his defense force. If not, all he would be able to do would be to try to lead the survivors overland to safety somewhere else.

Either way, though, he and the Gypsy would have to clean the place out before anything could be done. And to do that, they had to wait.

It wasn't easy for them to sit and watch while the Serbs looted and plundered the village. For the most part, the Serbs had it all their way, and several short bursts of gunfire echoed across the valley floor throughout the day.

Any damage to the village seemed to be selective. A couple of buildings went up in flames, but the Serbs made sure that the fires didn't spread. They would be living there and wouldn't want to see their new winter quarters destroyed.

ONCE NIGHT FELL, Bolan and his two companions left the ridge and made their way down to the valley floor. Leaving Petrova and the Gypsy under cover at the base of the hill, the Executioner slowly and carefully made his way into the heart of the village. He had left his night-vision goggles in the small room where he'd been staying, but the moon cast enough light for him to see by.

As he was unarmed, the first order of business was to find a weapon.

Along with pulling in all of their outposts, the Serbs hadn't bothered to set proper sentries. Bolan noted only two men wandering around inside the village proper. When the first sentry walked behind a house, Bolan was on him like a mountain lion.

Clamping his right hand over his mouth, he slammed his knee into the small of the man's back, at the same time smashing the edge of his left hand into his victim's neck behind his ear.

The Serb dropped to his knees without a sound, then slumped forward onto his face in the dirt.

After pausing to make sure that no one had heard him, Bolan rolled the body into the shadows before stripping it. He shrugged into the man's chest-pack magazine carrier and stuck his bayonet into his belt. After cracking the bolt to make sure that the AK-47 had a round in the chamber, he got to his feet.

Bolan found the doctor sleeping in the hut that had been given to him as a makeshift infirmary. Both of the cots were occupied, as was most of the floor, with injured villagers. Kubura himself was sleeping in the doorway as if trying to guard his patients.

The big American knelt beside the sleeping man. "Are you ready to fight yet, Doctor?" he whispered.

12

Kubura woke instantly at the sound of Bolan's voice. "Where did you come from?" he asked.

Bolan put his finger to his lips and motioned for Kubura to follow him outside. Once they were away from the houses, the Executioner crouched in the shadows and pulled the doctor down beside him. "Nina, the Gypsy and I are ready to put an end to this and free these people. Are you with us this time, or are you going to betray me to the Serbs again?"

Kubura took a deep breath to steady himself. If the soldier wanted payback, there was little he would be able to do about it. "I'm ready to help you," he said. "I can't tell you how sorry I am."

Bolan cut him short. "That can wait. I need your help right now."

"What do you want me to do?"

"First, I need information," Bolan replied. "I need to know how many men Zhinkovitch left in the village and where they're sleeping."

"There are only eighteen or so here now," Kubura said. "The rest left this afternoon after they'd disarmed the villagers. I heard some of them say that Zhinkovitch intends to garrison about thirty men here to winter over, so I don't know when they're coming back."

Bolan smiled grimly. "I'll just concentrate on those he left behind."

The doctor was silent for a long moment. Evil had always been an abstract concept to him. Now evil had a face and it was the face of a grinning Serbian gunman. Zhinkovitch had gone back on his pledge to Kubura and had turned his troops loose on the villagers. Now he had a chance to redeem himself through Jordan's more pragmatic view of reality, and he intended to do everything he could to help him.

Kubura quickly related that the Serbs had set up their command post in the village's small tavern. "The rest," he said, "can be almost anywhere. Some of them have taken the men into the church and are guarding them there. Others are looting the houses and molesting the women."

"How many of the village men are dead?"

"I saw at least three bodies, but I think there are more than that."

"There are certain to be more. Even if they were taken completely by surprise, some of them would have fought.

"Go back to your hut," he told Kubura. "I'll do my job tonight, and you can do yours in the morning."

BOLAN WATCHED the Gypsy move like a shadow. His first target was a large house in the center of the village. The body of an older man lay crumpled on the ground outside the door, and Bolan was afraid that it was Vlady Adan, but he was too far away to ID him. He hoped the village chief had survived. He'd need him in the morning to help rally the survivors to action.

Initially he had wanted the Gypsy to act as backup while he and Petrova cleared the village, but the man suggested an alternative. "Let her be the backup," he said, his hand on the hilt of his knife. "I know my way around this place and I am good at what I do."

Bolan saw the logic in that and agreed. "Okay, I'll let you lead the way."

He handed Petrova the AK-47 and magazine carrier he had taken from the Serb sentry. He kept the bayonet that had been attached to the weapon. "Set up at the north end, and I'll go with the Gypsy. Make sure that you have a back door, though. If a firefight breaks out, start a diversion. Fire off a couple of magazines, then get out of there. We'll meet up with you at the sheep station at the base of the hill. If we're not there by first light, try to make it back to Sarajevo.''

Petrova nodded. She had wanted to work beside the big man, but she knew that his decision was tactically correct. The Gypsy had lived in the village for some time. He knew who lived in each of the houses and who was likely to be in the most danger. Plus they had to be silent, and knife work had never been one of her strong points.

Now that Bolan was seeing the Gypsy in action, he knew that he had made the right decision. The small man moved like he had spent his entire life in a commando unit. After clearing the window at the front of the house, he slid the blade of his dagger through the crack of the door opening. He then tripped the latch and let the door silently swing open of its own weight, before slipping through the entrance.

A few minutes later he emerged, holding up a finger. One down, another dozen or so to go.

The man pointed to a house with flower boxes under the windowsills. ''That is the home of Gregor Pinkovitch,'' he whispered. ''His wife is the best-looking woman in the village, and they have two daughters. Some of the gunmen are sure to be here tonight. I saw Gregor's body lying in the square.''

Bolan nodded grimly. ''I'll take this one.''

He had worked his way up to the corner of the house when the front door opened and a gunman stumbled out, his rifle held loosely in his hand.

Rising from a crouch, Bolan moved forward, then clamped his hand over the Serb's mouth as he drove the AK-47's bayonet straight into his heart. The man stiffened, and his eyes rolled back in his head. Shifting his grip to his victim's collar, Bolan lowered him to the ground and dragged him out of the way. He took the time to wipe the blood from the bayonet so it wouldn't make the plastic grip slippery, before going through the door.

What had been the kitchen was thoroughly trashed. Food scraps, broken plates and empty liquor bottles littered the table and floor.

Around the corner of the bedroom door, Bolan saw a Serb passed out on the floor by the foot of the bed. The body of an older woman lay on the floor beside him, her neck twisted at an impossible angle.

On the bed, another Serb lay snoring next to a naked teenaged girl. Her face was bruised, and blood trickled from the corner of her mouth. When she looked up and saw Bolan in the doorway, she didn't scream. She was too far gone for that. Putting his finger to his lips and shaking his head, he signaled for the girl to keep quiet.

She watched, wide-eyed, as he stepped past the man on the floor, going for the one on the bed first. Leaning over him, Bolan placed his left hand over the sleeping man's mouth at the same time as he drove the knife into the hollow of his throat and up, to sever his brain stem at the base of his skull. The Serb's eyes flashed open, then immediately glazed over in death.

The one passed out on the floor wasn't a problem either, and Bolan made short work of him, as well. They deserved no mercy and none was given.

When the Serb's feet quit kicking, Bolan tossed the girl a blanket that had been kicked off the bed, motioning for her to remain silent and to stay in the house. She nodded her understanding as she scrambled out of the bed and climbed up into the bedroom loft over the main room.

Once outside the house, Bolan held up two fingers and the Gypsy nodded before moving on to his next target. Again, the small man slipped inside like a wraith and was back outside in a few minutes.

PETROVA WAITED ALONE in the darkness while Bolan and the Gypsy swept through the village like avenging angels. Once or twice she had seen them as they went from one house to the next and had caught the signals they gave each other. Even though they were going up against strong odds, she knew that they would prevail simply because Mack Bolan wouldn't accept defeat.

There was something about the big American that she had never seen in any other man. She almost felt sorry for the hapless Serbs who would be meeting their deaths at his hands. They had no idea who they were dealing with.

DAWN WAS ON THE WAY when Bolan and his companion finally arrived at the tavern in the center of the village that the Serbs had taken over as their command post. By now, both were armed with AK-47s, and Bolan had found some hand grenades. Since the men in the tavern were the last Serbs left alive in Valliskya, the need for silent killing was over.

Kicking the door open, Bolan and the Gypsy rushed into the room. Only the man seated at the table with a radio was awake. He went for his weapon, but Bolan triggered a single shot that sent him tumbling backward from the chair. Three other men were startled awake to find AK-47 muzzles trained on them.

"Do not shoot, soldier," one of the Serbs said as he raised his hands. "We surrender."

"Get facedown on the floor," Bolan barked.

The men quickly assumed the position.

"Go get Nina and the doctor," Bolan told his companion. "We've got a lot of work to do before the sun comes up."

13

When the sun rose over the valley, the full extent of the damage to the once-peaceful village of Valliskya could be clearly seen. Smoke rose from the burned houses and bodies lay on the ground, both victims of Zhinkovitch's rampaging gunmen and the Serbs Bolan and the Gypsy had cut down.

The villagers moved through the area, comforting the survivors and carrying the injured to Kubura's infirmary, which had been relocated to the larger tavern, where he attended to them with what few medicines he had left.

Bolan and the Gypsy had left no Serbs alive, except for the three they captured in the tavern. They were under guard, digging graves for their victims and for their late comrades.

The casualty list among the villagers was high. Half a dozen men had been killed, along with several women and a couple of the older children. The village chief's face was lined with grief as he gazed at the blanket-covered forms awaiting burial. One of those still forms was that of his wife, while another was that of one of his grandsons.

He sought out Bolan.

"All my life I have tried to avoid the hatred that has been the ruin of this land," Adan said. "I came here with my family so I would not have to fight."

"I am sorry that we brought this upon you," Bolan said, Petrova translating for him. "If we had not come here, this would not have happened."

"You did not create the ancient hatred that caused this to happen, nor did you create that monster Zhinkovitch. Me—" his thumb stabbed at his chest "—and others like me, created him because we did not have the courage to stand up against him when we could have stopped him. We let evil live, and now it has grown to this. We have no one to blame but ourselves."

Bolan didn't reply. He knew that there was a lot of truth in what Adan said. It never did any good to ignore evil and hope that it would go away by itself. Evil had to be faced head-on and fought wherever it was found.

"Now we will all fight," Adan said, "myself included. We will fight like free men should."

His dark eyes fixed on Bolan. "You are a soldier, and I know that you thought me a coward because I would not fight. I may have been a coward before, but I will not be a slave. Tell me what you want me to do and I will see that every man, woman and child in this village does exactly as you say."

"You had better think carefully about that," Bolan said. "There is no way that I can promise that more of your people won't die. It might be better if they packed their things and tried to escape."

Adan shook his head. "That we will not do. We will not live as slaves for a madman, and we will not run again. We will live or we will die where we are, but we will do it as a free people."

"You are certain of that?"

"I am certain."

At Adan's words, grim smiles of agreement broke out on the faces of some of the young men. Many of them had also lost loved ones or had been forced to watch as their women had been raped. They wanted payback.

"Okay," Bolan said, "if that is going to be the program, the first thing we need to do is to see how many weapons we have left and how much ammunition there is for them. Then I need to talk to your best hunters and any of your men who have had military training.''

"I have several good hunters," Adan said, "but not many of the men have served in the army."

"Just send me those who have had even a little military experience, and I will use them to help train the rest. Also, I want to use the Gypsy as my second in command with Nina."

Adan's eyes flickered over to the man, who was walking toward them. "He is not of our people, but he is a good man and my people will obey him, as they will you," he said firmly. "I will see to that."

"Zhinkovitch's men didn't take the guns with them when they left," the Gypsy announced when he reached them. "They were all gathered and stacked in the back of the tavern."

Bolan smiled for the first time. "Pass them out, then let's start getting our defenses set up again. We have a lot to do and not much time in which to do it."

"I also have the radio," the Gypsy said, "and it seems to be working."

"Ask if there is anyone who knows how to operate a radio," Bolan told Petrova.

"I do," a young man said in English. "I was a radioman in the Croatian army before I came here."

"Good. I want you to monitor the radio and try to answer any calls that come in. I don't know if these men were supposed to make scheduled reports to Zhinkovitch, so you'll have to do the best you can."

"In the army," the radioman said, "an outpost like this would have been expected to make two calls a day, one at noon and one at midnight. I can make those calls."

"We don't know the call sign, though."

The man smiled grimly. "I think I can get the call signs from one of those men you captured."

"All right," Bolan said, "let's get to work."

As SOON AS the last of the graves had been dug, Bolan put his Serb prisoners to work digging fighting positions. At first, he had simple foxholes dug, spaced well apart along a perimeter that encompassed the whole village. If they had the time later, they could be expanded with supplemental positions, connecting trenches and overhead cover.

While that was going on, Bolan and the Gypsy formed six squads from the most able-bodied men in the village. With Adan's help, he chose squad leaders for each unit. The older men and boys too young to be in the squads—some twenty all told—were organized into a reserve platoon and armed with the bolt-action rifles.

Once everyone was armed, Bolan made the defensive sector assignments. He assigned three squads to be on duty at any one time, while the other three would either be sleeping or working on the fighting positions.

Leaving Petrova with the work party, he and the Gypsy took the first of the squads outside the perimeter and set up a makeshift range south of the village. Empty kerosene tins and small barrels were set up at a hundred yards for targets. Giving each man twenty rounds, they started showing them how to use the AK-47s.

BY EVENING, Bolan had the rudiments of a defense set up. Fighting positions had been dug every ten yards or so all the way around the village. The hunters and military veterans Adan had pointed out had been armed and set out in the hills to act as early-warning sentries. If they spotted the Serbs returning, they were to fire warning shots, then get back to the village without trying to stop them.

The night passed uneventfully, and Bolan had little to do except walk the perimeter and check his sentries.

When the false dawn came, Bolan finally called it quits.

Soon afterward, Nina Petrova went to Bolan's room.

"I have everyone standing to," she said.

"Good." He winced as he reached for his boots.

"How is your leg?" she asked.

"Better," he replied, flexing his thigh. Kubura had done a good job repairing the damage and, even with the extra exertion he had given it in the last two days, it seemed to be healing well.

"Do you think this is going to work?" Petrova asked.

"To be honest with you, I don't know. It's going to depend mostly on the villagers. If they fight hard enough, they stand a chance. If they break and run, though, it'll be over pretty quickly. There's no way that the three of us can win a stand-up fight against those kind of odds."

"Promise me something?" she said.

"What's that?"

"Do not let them take me alive."

Bolan didn't have to ask her what she meant. He knew how prevalent the gang rape of women prisoners was.

"I won't let them take you if I can help it," he assured her. "But make sure that you have a pistol with you at all times."

She opened her coat to show him the butt of a 7.62 mm Tokarev stuck in her belt. "I always scored high on the pistol range," she said with a grim smile, "so I do not think I will miss my own head."

"I'll have to make sure that it doesn't come to that."

LATER THAT MORNING, Bolan and his two companions inspected their fighting positions.

"Why do they not come?" Petrova asked as she looked out past the outer defenses. "This waiting is worse than the fighting."

"Waiting is always worse," Bolan said. "The longer we have to wait for something to happen, the better it is for Zhinkovitch. The villagers will start getting nervous and maybe think that they really don't want to do things this way. It's psychological warfare, the oldest game in the world, and it always works to the attacker's advantage."

"I will make sure that they do not change their minds," the Gypsy said. "We have gone too far to turn back now."

"Don't be too hard on them," Bolan advised, "but don't let them talk one another into a panic either. I think we can hold on here as long as they don't lose their heads."

"The only thing they will talk about when I am around is killing Serbs."

"Remember that many of them are Serbs, too."

"That is not an easy thing to forget."

Bolan shook his head. Even when they had to fight together or die, the age-old ethnic divisions weren't something that could be put aside.

"Just see that it doesn't get in the way of what has to be done here."

"It will not," the man promised. "Even I know that there are a few good Serbs."

14

Throughout the day, Bolan continued organizing the squads while the rest of the villagers dug more fighting positions and connecting trenches. With the basic perimeter defenses established, he was able to have timber and earth placed over some of the positions to turn them into bunkers. Unlike the day before, the mood of the people was lighter. Seeing their men armed again and the defenses being built was giving them hope that they could survive.

One by one, Bolan and the Gypsy took the squads out to the firing range for more training. Since he had commandeered the ammunition supplies Zhinkovitch's men had had with them, Bolan had quite a few more rounds to use. The more familiar the men were with their weapons, the more effectively they would use them when the time came.

The Croatian who had volunteered to man the radio hadn't been able to fool the communications center in Zhinkovitch's fortress for very long. He had been able to get past the first radio check by saying that the regular radio operator had been too drunk to call in. By evening, though, the comm center had demanded to speak to Lazar, and when the Croatian hadn't been able to bring him to the radio, the comm center had cut off abruptly.

Zhinkovitch had to know that something was wrong. Bolan could only hope that it would take the warlord at least a day to investigate.

IT WAS LATE AFTERNOON, and Bolan was inspecting the roof on the first bunker when he heard a single warning shot from the men watching the approaches.

The Gypsy raced toward him. "Soldier," he called out, pointing to the hills, "we have visitors coming!"

Bolan saw a group of six riders approaching, flying a white flag. Judging from the bulk of the man on the lead horse, it could only be Dushan Zhinkovitch.

"We'll go out to meet them," he said, slinging his assault rifle. "I don't want to let him inside our defenses. It looks pretty good from the outside, but I don't want him inside where he can spot our weaknesses."

"I will come with you," Adan said through Petrova. "I want him to see that we are united in this effort."

As they rode closer, Bolan noted that Zhinkovitch's men had their AK-47s slung across their backs and were being careful to keep their hands in sight. The warlord was armed only with his dagger and a pistol in his belt, but he seemed unconcerned by the weapons pointed at him. One thing Bolan had to give him was that he knew how to play the psychological game well.

"That's close enough, Zhinkovitch," Bolan called out, his hand wrapped around the pistol grip of his weapon. "We can talk here."

The escort halted, but Zhinkovitch nudged his mount a few steps closer to Bolan. "I badly underestimated you, soldier," he said, "and it has cost me. I will make sure that I do not do that again."

Bolan met his gaze squarely. "All you have to do is leave these people in peace, and you'll have no more trouble from me. I don't want to make war with you, but I want these people left alone."

The Serb shook his head. "I do not understand you, soldier. What do you care about these peasants? They are not Americans. What happens to them is not your concern, but mine. They can stay here and work their lands as they have always done. The only difference will be that they will work for me. They are peasants, and they have to work for somebody.''

"I've seen what happens to people who work for you, as you put it," Bolan replied. "I can't allow that to happen here. You have other villages supporting you and you do not need these people."

"These peasants killed my men," Zhinkovitch said. "What kind of a leader would I be if I did nothing about that?"

"I killed your men myself," Bolan said, his hand ready to go for his weapon. "So you can take that one up with me alone."

"I also do not want a war with you, soldier," Zhinkovitch said. "I will make the same generous offer to you that I made before. You and the woman can go free, but Dr. Kubura stays with me."

"And the villagers?"

"Like I said, they have to work for someone. After you and the woman are gone, they will work for me."

"That's not good enough," Bolan stated. "I don't leave here unless I have your word that these people will be free to live their lives in peace."

Zhinkovitch shook his head slowly. "You are dreaming soldier. Peace in this land does not come so easily. It is what men like me make. You are an American, so you probably do not understand that easily. I will give you more time to think about it. I will come back tomorrow morning for your decision. Sleep well tonight, if you can."

Without waiting for a reply, the warlord reined his horse around and rode off.

The Gypsy spit on the ground. He would have preferred to kill Zhinkovitch while they had the chance, but the big American wanted to play this by his rules. The Gypsy wondered if they were making a big mistake.

"WHY IS HE WAITING until tomorrow?" Petrova asked. "He has enough men to attack us now."

"It's part of the game," Bolan said. "He doesn't want to risk his people more than he has to. The longer he waits, the greater the chance that the villagers will back down."

"So we wait some more," Petrova said.

"No," Bolan announced, "we're not going to wait and play his game. I'm going to play *my* game and go after him tonight. Gypsy, I want you to pick five of your best men, and arm them with AK-47s and as many hand grenades as we can spare.''

''And their knives, too,'' the small man said.

''Yes. Nina, I want you to stay here in case we need fire support to cover us on the way back in. I don't trust the locals not to shoot us up in the dark.''

Although she would rather have gone with the raiding party, Petrova was too disciplined to protest. They had placed their fate in Bolan's hands, and she knew the only way they were going to survive was if they followed his orders.

BOLAN HAD THE POINT position as his small raiding force crept up on the Serbian camp in the dark. The gunmen had made their camp on the flat, a mile and a half to the west where the trail came down from the hills. It was a good campsite, but awkward to defend because it didn't offer good observation of the approaches.

Zhinkovitch had put a few sentries out to guard the perimeter. It was well after midnight, and there had been no major activity in the camp for well over an hour. The Gypsy was close behind Bolan when the Executioner spotted the sentry along their approach route. Without a word, he pointed toward the Serb, then drew his index finger across his own throat. The little man nodded, his hand already moving to the hilt of the dagger in his belt. Bolan held his position, his rifle at the ready, as the Gypsy disappeared into the darkness.

While he waited for his companion to take out his target, Bolan scoped out the enemy camp. Except for the sentry, there was no one between him and what he figured were the supply tents. The big man intended to destroy as much of their supplies as possible. Although he knew that the warlord would be able to replace what he destroyed, it would hinder his assault and buy Bolan some time.

The sentry suddenly disappeared from sight. Two minutes later, the Gypsy returned. Bolan signaled for the five villagers to move up to join them.

The Executioner had given the men specific assignments. Three of them carried torches that, once lit, would be used to set the camp on fire. Bolan, the Gypsy and the other two villagers would cover their withdrawal and inflict what damage they could on any pursuers.

Halting at the edge of the encampment, Bolan motioned for the men with the torches to move forward. There was a fire burning in front of the first tent, and the torchmen quickly ignited their oil-and-rag torches. As soon as they were blazing, they took off running through the camp, stopping only to set their flame to anything they found that would burn.

His sights fixed on the ammunition supply tent to the side, Bolan pulled the pin on a grenade and tossed the bomb through the open flap. The tent erupted with a series of explosions, which brought the Serbian gunmen charging out of their tents. Silhouetted against the fires the torchmen had set, they made good targets. Bolan snapped off a quick 3-round burst at the first man. Without waiting to see him go down, he cut loose again.

This time, his fire was returned as the Serbs got to their weapons. For a few moments, rounds flew erratically as the gunmen fought shadows. The three torchmen had disappeared into the darkness, their mission complete.

The Gypsy and his two men had gone deeper into the camp. Seeing them drawing fire, Bolan ripped off the rest of his magazine into the center of the camp. He then pulled his last grenade, armed the bomb and hurled it as far as he could.

As soon as it detonated, the Serbs went to ground and the squad made good its escape. The Gypsy was the last man to make it out, and he emerged carrying an RP-46 machine gun.

"Did everyone get out?" Bolan asked him.

"No, we lost one, but no one else was hit."

"Move out and I'll cover you."

Packing his prize, the Gypsy took off into the night.

ZHINKOVITCH KICKED the body of a villager, driving the toe of his boot into the dead man's ribs with a thud. The gray light of early dawn showed him the full extent of the damage that had been done by the soldier's midnight raid, and he felt a need to take his anger out on someone, or something, until he could get his hands on the American.

Not satisfied with breaking the corpse's ribs, Zhinkovitch brought his foot up again before slamming it into the side of the skull. This time, the smashing of the corpse's temple seemed to assuage some of his anger.

He looked over what remained of his camp. Thin tendrils of smoke rose from some of the burned-out tents, while those that still stood had been shot up. A body lay on the ground, awaiting disposal.

He hadn't expected this. The soldier had obviously been able to put some backbone into those peasants, but it would do them no good in the long run. They had been able to pull off a sneak night attack like thieves, but there was no way that they could stand up to a concentrated attack.

The platoon leader he had appointed to take Lazar's place as his second in command approached. The loss of Lazar was something for which the soldier would pay dearly. Lazar had been a good man, with him from the very beginning.

"There are eight dead, Chief," the man reported, "and another five wounded. It looks like they took one of the machine guns and at least one grenade launcher."

"It does not matter what they took," the warlord said. "It will do them no good. I will crush them all now, the doctor included. No one does something like this to Dushan Zhinkovitch and lives to talk about it. Get your things together, then get the men ready to attack."

"We are going to need ammunition," the platoon leader said. "The men have only the magazines they were carrying in their pouches. Everything else was burned or blown up."

"Get more ammunition sent out from the fortress, but I am not going to wait for it. We are going to attack this morning even if the men have to do it with their bare hands."

"I will tell them, Chief."

"Make sure they know that if they let those peasants stop them, they will suffer for it. I will not have people like them think that they can do this to me. They must be punished for what they have done."

15

The sun hadn't yet cleared the mountaintops when Bolan called a meeting with Petrova, the Gypsy, Vlady Adan and the squad leaders. Even though one man had been lost in the attack, the villagers had taken the success of the raid as a sign that they had the upper hand. The Executioner knew that he had to bring them back to the reality of the situation.

"The people are excited," Adan said to Bolan through Petrova. "You showed them that they can fight back at the Serbs and win."

"We cannot let our guard down," Bolan cautioned. "All I did was buy us some time. There were not enough of us to really hurt him."

"Can you take more men tonight and try to do it again?" Adan asked.

Bolan shook his head. "No. That was the kind of surprise attack that only works once. He will have all his men on guard tonight, and we would never get through his perimeter. We are not going to be able to pull any more tricks like that. We are going to have to stand and fight when he comes the next time. All we can do now is get ready for him.''

Adan nodded. Like Bolan, he knew the value of keeping everyone focused on the task at hand.

''Keep the villagers digging more fighting positions,'' Bolan told him. ''We need them more than anything else right now, apart from luck and more ammunition.''

He turned to the Gypsy. ''Find me two men who know how to shoot an RPG and two men to go with them as loaders. It's time to get moving.''

THE GYPSY HAD CLAIMED the RP-46 machine gun he had brought back as his own. Fortunately not all of the 7.62 mm rimmed ammunition had been stripped from the machine-gun belts for the rifles, so with the one ammo can he had grabbed with the gun, he had almost two thousand rounds for it. He intended to put every last one of them to good use.

''Do you know how to use that thing?'' Bolan asked.

The Gypsy stopped polishing the inside of the machine gun's feed tray and grinned. ''I can make one of these sing a song you have never heard before."

Bolan studied the smaller man for a long moment. "You're an interesting man, Gypsy."

"So are you. You and I will sit down with a bottle of brandy when this is all over, and we will tell each other the stories of our lives."

Bolan gave a half smile. "Perhaps we will."

Leaving the man to finish cleaning his prize, Bolan went to inspect their other spoils of war. They now had three RPG-7 antitank rocket launchers and two dozen 85 mm rockets for them.

Calling Petrova over, Bolan told her what he needed to convert the rockets. A few minutes later, two of the village's boys approached him, one carrying a bucket full of gravel, the other a box of small nails.

Bolan carefully pried off the ballistic nose cone of the antitank rockets with the blade of a bayonet, exposing the empty inverted cone of the shaped-charge warhead. He then filled the empty cone with nails and gravel before snapping the nose cone back in place. He knew this would increase the warhead's fragmentation effect tenfold. When one of the rockets was detonated, it would go off like a Claymore mine, spraying rocks and nails in a shotgunlike blast. It was a bit crude and he would have liked to have had steel balls to use for the shrapnel, and clay or plaster to keep them in place. But they would work, and that was all that really mattered.

He was almost finished doctoring the last of the RPG rockets when Petrova walked up and knelt beside him.

"Some of the women have asked me if they could be given weapons so they can fight, too. They want to strike back at the men who defiled them."

"They can use any extra bolt-action rifles we have. I don't want them using the AK-47s and burning up a lot of ammo on full-auto."

"I will be glad to show them how to shoot the rifles," she volunteered.

"Good," Bolan said, remembering that she, too, had a personal score to settle.

By MIDMORNING, Bolan had laid out his defense plan, and his forces were deployed and ready for Zhinkovitch to make his next move. It was an odd feeling for him to be reacting to a military situation, and it had been some time since he had fought a defensive battle. A commando raid or an ambush wasn't quite the same as commanding almost a hundred men in the defense of a built-up area.

Bolan knew well the first rule of warfare: no plan ever survived the first contact with the enemy. It was also the last rule. There was always the chance that his squads wouldn't be able to stand up under a determined assault.

He did have the advantage of fighting on home turf, or at least, the home turf of his fighters. While Zhinkovitch's men were fighting for loot or because they feared their leader, his men and women were fighting for their homes and their lives. Whether it would make enough of a difference was yet to be seen. But without that psychological edge, he knew the villagers wouldn't have a chance.

"Here they come," Bolan said to Petrova.

A skirmish line was slowly working its way toward them. The camouflaged Serbs were bunched up, rather than spread out, like more experienced troops would have been. That was going to work for the Executioner in their first attack, but he expected that they would learn quickly when they saw what they were up against.

"Pass the word for everyone to hold their fire and let them come in close," Bolan told Petrova. "Let them get right up on top of us before anyone fires. We need to kill as many of them as we can in the first volley."

The big American walked over to the bunker with the RP-46 machine gun. He checked the ammunition belt and got ready for his part in the battle. If the Gypsy and his men did their bit, they stood a chance of pulling it off.

THE GYPSY AND HIS two handpicked RPG gunners hid in the hayloft of a small wooden barn just beyond the perimeter defenses and watched as the Serbs approached the village.

The small man had thought that the barn would have made a good place for the RP-46 machine gun he had acquired, but the American had insisted that the gun be left in the bunker. The Gypsy had the old, long-barreled Mosin-Nagant the soldier had found, along with his AK-47. A long time ago, his father had had such a rifle, and he had learned to hunt with it as a boy.

Running the rifle sight up to twelve hundred meters, the Gypsy sighted in on the man with the radio at the rear of the attacking force. It was time to put his old hunting skills to work.

16

The village looked deserted when Zhinkovitch scanned it through his field glasses as his troops advanced. He knew, however, that it wasn't. The soldier was down there waiting for him, along with his armed rabble. The peasants were hardly worthy opponents, but the Serb knew now that he couldn't discount the effect the soldier was having on them. The raid on his camp the previous night had driven that point home all too clearly.

He didn't regret having given the soldier a chance to go free when he could have killed him. There were those who would have said that he had been much too generous, particularly in allowing the Russian woman to go with him. But he had admired the soldier's boldness and had done it as a gesture from one fighting man to another. Now that his generosity had been turned against him, though, he would get his revenge.

When he was finished with the village of Valliskya, no one would dare lift their hand against Dushan Zhinkovitch again.

"Tell them to move in faster," he told the radioman standing behind him. The sooner they got started, the sooner he would be able to exact his vengeance.

FOR BOLAN'S PLAN to work, the Gypsy and his RPG gunners had to wait until Zhinkovitch's men were completely committed to the attack. If they fired the rockets too soon, much of the shock effect of the doctored warheads would be wasted.

Bolan regretted not having radios. To make up for the communications deficit, he had placed stakes, to which rags had been tied, in the center of a number of sectioned-off areas. Similar stakes had been put up in the other sectors. They were integral to the tactic the Executioner had decided to employ: defending the village sector by sector, stretching their forces to the maximum.

He knew that he would be able to run this sector defense game only as long as Zhinkovitch played along with him. As soon as the warlord figured out that a two-pronged attack would split their defenses, he would lose the ability to concentrate his forces. Right now, though, the Serbs were cooperating with his plan, and he couldn't ask for any more than that.

THE GYPSY HAD the sight blade of the old Mosin-Nagant rifle centered on the radioman when the lead man of the attacking force drew even with the stake in the middle of the killing zone. It was time to spring the soldier's trap.

"Fire," he told the first RPG gunner as he tightened his finger on the rifle's trigger.

The sound of the rifle's report was lost in the whoosh of the rocket leaving the launcher. Since the 7.62 mm round traveled faster than the rocket, the radiomen had fallen before the RPG round hit.

The effect of Bolan's modified warhead was spectacular. When the charge detonated, it blew out the double handful of gravel and nails like a giant sawed-off shotgun blast. The shrapnel took out half a dozen men in the front rank, while cutting up several others in the rear.

No sooner had the first rocket detonated than the second one was sent on its way.

Zhinkovitch's forces went to ground. Since it was impossible to hide the back blast of the grenade launcher, they knew exactly where Bolan's men were firing from. A storm of lead slashed into the old barn.

The weathered boards offered no protection against the 7.62 mm rounds. Bullets snapped over the Gypsy's head, sending splinters flying. The small man knew that if the gunners tried to fire again, they would be cut down.

"Run!" he shouted to his gunners. He shifted his aiming point to give the retreating men a little covering fire. The Mosin-Nagant fired again and a Serb, ready to fire his own RPG in return, keeled over facefirst. It was too late to stop the launcher. The misaimed rocket drove into the ground a few feet in front of the dead gunner then detonated, taking a few Serb gunmen as victims.

Working the bolt to chamber a new round, the Gypsy scanned the battlefield. He would stay where he was as long as he could, to draw fire away from the RPG gunners so they could make it back to the perimeter. He targeted a Serb gunman. Gently squeezing the trigger, he was rewarded by seeing the man go down with a 7.62 mm round in the chest.

WITH THE SERB ATTACK stalled in front of the barn, Bolan knew it was time to start breaking them up. He picked up the loaded RPG launcher and thumbed back the firing hammer. Aiming the rocket at the center of the attackers, he pulled the trigger. Once again, the doctored rocket warhead chewed into a number of Serbs with a single blast. Quickly loading another round into the front of the launcher, he sighted it and fired again.

Without wasting time to see the rocket hit its target, the Executioner took the RPG launcher and ran down the trench to the machine gun he'd made the Gypsy leave behind. The rockets had done their work, and now it was time to see if he could clear out Zhinkovitch's troops with a little concentrated machine-gun fire.

Settling in behind the RP-46, Bolan flipped up the sight, ran the side bar up to the four hundred meter mark and started snapping out controlled 6-round bursts. Shooting that way instead of lying down on the trigger not only conserved precious ammunition, but kept the gun's barrel from overheating. Since he didn't have a spare barrel for the machine gun, he needed to conserve it as much as he could.

All along the front, Bolan could tell that the villagers were getting in their licks, too, the chatter of AK-47s and barks of the Mosin-Nagant rifles sounding over the hammering of the RP-46.

The Serbs weren't pulling back, though. One of the warlord's squad leaders tried to storm the perimeter. A sustained burst of riflefire put paid to his efforts, taking two of his men with him and sending the rest of the squad scattering.

THE GYPSY RAMMED another clip of five 7.62 mm cartridges into the top of the open action of the Mosin-Nagant rifle and shoved the rounds into the built-in magazine. Pulling the empty clip free, he closed the bolt to chamber a round. He knew it was almost time for him to get back inside the perimeter.

The soldier's machine-gun fire was forcing the Serbs to keep their heads down, but the Gypsy noticed a couple of them trying to make their way around to the side of the barn. He fixed one in his sight and fired. The man screamed, then fell back.

Slinging the long rifle, the small man picked up his AK-47 and flicked the selector switch to full-auto. He would need the firepower.

Moving to the back of the hayloft, he dropped to the ground. He picked his way through the stored farm equipment, then slipped out of the barn and into the tall grass.

FROM THE RIDGE LINE overlooking the village, Dushan Zhinkovitch watched the battle below with barely controlled rage. The soldier was making a complete fool of him. The killing zone he had drawn his men into was the work of a professional, and the warlord had to admire it. There was nothing for them to do for now but to withdraw while they still could.

"Tell them to pull back," he told his radio operator.

"I cannot reach anyone, Chief," the radio operator said a few seconds later. "No one is answering."

Zhinkovitch had seen the sniper in the barn taking out his squad leaders. He realized belatedly that he had probably also shot all of his radiomen.

He was almost relieved when he saw his men start to fall back of their own accord. They weren't losing control, but were withdrawing like trained soldiers, which made him feel a little better. Nevertheless, their withdrawal twisted in his gut like a knife.

As ZHINKOVITCH'S men turned back, Bolan fired one last burst from the machine gun. Slowly the firing from the perimeter ceased as well.

Bolan was in the machine-gun bunker loading ammunition belts into the can beside the breech of the RP-46, when Petrova found him. She muttered something in Russian as she looked out past the perimeter.

"What does that mean?" Bolan asked.

"It's an old Russian proverb. The best way to defend is to attack."

"We say the best defense is a strong offense, but it means the same thing. It seems to have worked this time at least."

"Now what do we do?"

"We get ready for the next attack," Bolan said. "We did a good job this time, considering what we had to work with. But we haven't seen the last of Zhinkovitch. I'm hoping he'll throw a night attack at us."

"Why is that?"

"Night attacks are pretty confusing for both sides, so the defender has the advantage as he is on his home ground. Even though experienced troops can handle night attacks, the villagers know the area better than the Serbs do, and I have to make that work for us.

"But it won't matter if we have to go through many more attacks. We're too short on weapons and ammunition to keep this up for very long. I've instructed the Gypsy to collect ammunition and weapons from the dead gunmen, which will help, but we still don't have enough to waste. All

Zhinkovitch has to do is to keep throwing attacks against us, and we'll use it up real fast.''

''But it is over for now, is it not?''

''Yes, it is,'' Bolan agreed, ''but the work isn't. I want the men back to work on the defenses and on the lookout for snipers.

Kubura was surprised at how few villagers had been shot during the attack. Only two men had come to him, and both of their wounds had been relatively light.

The other thing that surprised him was how well the villagers were handling this. He had expected them to be as affected as the people he had seen in Sarajevo, but they were showing fierce determination and a desire to make the warlord pay for invading their lives. They were acting like they actually expected to beat him.

Regardless of what they thought, Kubura expected things to only get worse. As good as Jordan was, the doctor couldn't believe, however much he wanted to, that he was going to be able to defeat Zhinkovitch and his bandit army. There were simply too many Serbs and they were too well equipped.

People were going to die, and there was nothing he could do about it.

17

Zhinkovitch surveyed the battlefield. The bodies of his men lay where they had fallen during the abortive attack, and he could see the villagers moving over them, looting for ammunition and supplies. It made him want to spit to see those filthy peasants stealing from him.

He had to admit that he had badly underestimated the soldier again. He knew that he had made a major mistake letting him go when he had had him in his hands. It was a mistake he wouldn't make twice. The next time he had his hands on the soldier, he was going to see to it that the American took a long time dying. A very long time.

For now, though, he had to concern himself with the problem at hand. The soldier had built up a formidable defense that had to be reduced before he could get to him. The previous attack had shown that he needed heavy weapons to do that job.

"Call back to the base and have them send up two of the 82 mm mortars," he ordered one of his gunmen.

"Yes, Chief."

The soldier was good, but how well would his peasant army stand up against mortar fire? When the mortars started to fall, the soldier's rabble would throw down their weapons and run in terror.

But that wouldn't save them. He had decided that he was going to hunt down each one of them—man, woman and child—and make an example of them. He would have their bodies impaled on stakes for the ravens to eat.

He smiled to himself when he imagined the valley below dotted with rotting corpses. His men would grumble about the extra work, but it would be worthwhile. The mountain people would remember him forever.

THE VILLAGERS WERE more subdued as night fell. The euphoria of having beaten back Zhinkovitch's attack had given way to the realization that one battle didn't end a war. As long as the warlord's troops were out there, they were in danger.

Bolan assessed the spoils of the raid. More than a dozen weapons, mostly AK-47s, and as many magazine carriers, and at least two dozen hand grenades had been salvaged from the bodies of Zhinkovitch's men. It wasn't much, but it would replace some of the ammunition they'd used up in the attack.

Some of the younger men had also stripped the camouflage jackets from the Serbs and were wearing them.

"I know that wearing camouflage makes them think that they are soldiers," Bolan said to Adan through Petrova, "but all it is going to do is to get them shot by mistake. Also, we need to make sure that no lights are showing anywhere tonight. We have to be completely blacked out so we do not provide Zhinkovitch with any targets.

"He is a good man to have in charge of the village," Petrova said as she watched Adan walk off to give the orders.

"They could do with someone like him in Sarajevo to clean up the UN," Bolan said, then he smiled ruefully. "Unfortunately I don't think that will ever happen."

As soon as it was completely dark, Bolan called the Gypsy over. "I want to move that machine gun out of the bunker."

"But why? It worked well there today. I saw you kill several of the enemy with it."

"That is exactly why we have to move it," Bolan explained. "Now that the warlord and his men know where it is, it'll be their number one target. We're going to move it off to one side where it'll be able to cover the old bunker. That way, if they send in a team to take it out, we can bring them under fire."

The small man smiled. "I like the way you think, soldier. You have the devious mind of a Gypsy."

"Then we're going to put out some surprises in front of our positions."

Bolan picked up one of the grenades that had been collected from the battlefield. "I'm going to set out some booby traps as early-warning devices. They'll tell us when the Serbs are coming, and they might take out a few of them at the same time."

"How do we do this thing?"

Bolan quickly told him what he needed, and the Gypsy went to find the materials. It took a while to find something suitable with which to rig the booby trap trip wires. Finally someone came up with a roll of dark line that was strong enough for what Bolan had in mind. He also had a spool of heavy wire and a bundle of small sharpened stakes that had been holding up someone's tomato plants. It wasn't much, but he had managed before with less.

Bolan didn't have enough extra grenades to booby-trap all the approaches to the perimeter, so he concentrated on covering the most likely avenues. Starting far out so he could work his way back in without running into his own handiwork, he knelt beside the footpath leading into the village and took out a stake and the hammer. "We'll start here."

After hammering the first stake into the ground a yard off the side of the trail, he tied the line to it at ankle height. A yard off the other side of the trail, he hammered in the second stake. He then used the spool of wire to bind one of the Russian grenades to the stake, making sure that the safety spoon was free to move. Then he pulled the line across the trail and tied it to the pull ring on the safety pin of the grenade.

Stretched at ankle height, the line could barely be seen. Zhinkovitch's troops would have their eyes focused on the village in front of them, not at their feet. A boot catching the line would pull the pin out of the safety spoon, and the grenade would detonate four seconds later.

Bolan put the next booby trap a little closer toward the perimeter than the first. The third went in a hundred yards to the left along a path between two fields. When he was done, two dozen grenades had been set out to await the warlord's next move.

"Remember," he told the Gypsy when they were back inside the perimeter, "we can't go out there now, either. Those booby-trapped grenades will kill one of us as quickly as it will kill one of them. A booby trap has no friends."

"Just as long as they are not friendly to the Serbs," the Gypsy said.

"Believe me, they won't be."

BOLAN HAD GIVEN himself the midnight watch duty. He looked out over the fields beyond the perimeter. It was a different landscape, but the feeling was the same: waiting in the dark for an enemy he couldn't see was an old story, and it never got any better. He had told Petrova that the night favored the defender. In a conventional army that was true, but when you added in the terror of the unknown and working with untested troops, it tended to warp the results.

The hollow, coughing thunk of a mortar round leaving the tube was unmistakable. Zhinkovitch had gotten smart and raised the ante.

"Take cover!" Bolan yelled as he threw himself flat on the ground. "Mortars!"

In the flash from the detonation, he saw that someone got caught in the blast. Bolan picked himself up and ran the few yards to the closest fighting position.

By now, everyone had got under cover. There was a long pause before the next round, either a sign that the gun crew wasn't experienced or that it didn't have much ammunition. Either way, it was to Bolan's advantage.

As he cautiously looked out over the edge of the trench in which he had taken refuge, Petrova slid in beside him. Her AK-47 was slung over her shoulder, and she was wearing a chest-pack magazine carrier that had been taken from one of the dead Serbs. "What is he doing?"

"Exactly what I would be doing in the circumstances if I was him," Bolan replied. "He's making sure that we don't get any sleep."

"It's working," she said. "I've never been so scared."

Bolan understood only too well what it was like to come under indirect fire—no one to shoot back at and nothing to do but to duck and trust to luck. He knew that he had to find some way to distract Petrova.

"As soon as this attack is over, I want you to make your way to the next position and pass the word for everyone to remain on guard. Zhinkovitch could be using the mortars as cover fire for a simultaneous ground attack.''

Petrova nodded.

''Where is the Gypsy?'' Bolan asked.

''He is in the new bunker with the machine gun.''

''Stay here until this is over. I need to talk to him.''

''Be careful.''

''I will.''

Bolan waited until the next round detonated, then made a dash for the bunker.

The Gypsy was peering out through the firing port of the bunker, waiting for the Serbs to appear in front of his gun sights. His new position covered the flank of the old bunker, and he expected to make a good killing.

He turned when Bolan climbed through the back door of the bunker. ''That Serb bastard is getting smarter, and that is bad news for us,'' the small man said.

''He's probably going to hit us with a night attack as soon as he stops shelling us.''

''I'll be ready,'' the Gypsy said, patting the breech of the gun.

''Let them get in close,'' Bolan advised, ''but not too close. I'll be ready with the RPG launcher if they try to take you out.''

"I will deal with them," the Gypsy answered him.

THE MORTARS CONTINUED to fire for a little over an hour. The rounds were well spaced—one every three minutes or so—but thankfully they did little damage to the defenses. Several of the houses were hit, however, and the reserve platoon was kept busy taking the casualties to Kubura's makeshift operating room.

As suddenly as it had begun, the mortar barrage was over.

"Go now," Bolan told Petrova. "Pass the word for them to get ready."

Clutching her AK-47, the woman scrambled out of the trench and ran for the next position.

When nothing happened for several long minutes, Bolan began to think he had missed the call. He had to remind himself that Zhinkovitch wasn't the product of formal military training and couldn't be counted on to do what a trained military officer would do under the same circumstances.

Suddenly the night was shattered by the flash and explosion of one of the booby-trapped grenades. "They're coming," Bolan shouted.

He hadn't guessed wrong after all.

18

The second detonation brought a hail of full-auto fire slashing into the perimeter along a broad front. Most of the Serbs' rounds were aimed too high to be effective, though, and Bolan knew that if the villagers kept their heads down until the last possible moment before firing, they could beat off the attack.

The Gypsy tracked the lead elements of the attack in the sights of his machine gun by their muzzle-flashes. The Serbs had started firing too far out and he had them cold, but he also knew that the minute he opened up on them with the RP-46, he would become the center of a great deal of unwelcomed attention.

Bolan had told him to bail out if they got in too close, but there was no way that he was going to abandon the gun to be recaptured or destroyed. It was the only heavy weapon they had, and as long as he had ammunition belts for it, he was going to use it. He would wait as long as he could before firing, so that he wouldn't waste any of his precious ammunition. When he saw a Serb raise an RPG rocket launcher in his direction, though, he knew he couldn't wait any longer.

Pressing the trigger, he snapped out a short 6-round burst. The RPG gunner disappeared from target acquisition, and the Gypsy changed his aiming point to the lead elements of the assault before again laying down hard on the trigger. The 7.62 mm ammo belts were loaded with one tracer round for every four, and their orange streaks through the night let him see exactly where his rounds were striking. They also let the Serbs see his firing position.

One of the Serbs had tracers in his AK-47's magazine, and he began snapping out short bursts in the Gypsy's direction. As if on a signal, the others started to concentrate their fire on him, as well. Rifle rounds began to slam into the front of his bunker like a heavy rain. A tracer round flashed through the small firing port, missing his head by a fraction of an inch.

Swinging the gun to the right, the Gypsy zeroed in on the man with the tracers and gave him a short burst. He didn't see his rounds connect, but the tracer fire ceased.

FROM HIS FIGHTING hole several yards away, Bolan saw the enemy fire converging on the Gypsy's bunker. As he'd expected, it was drawing them in like flies. Knowing that he had to divert their attention and draw some of the fire from the bunker, he picked up the RPG launcher. He had a good side deflection shot at their flank, and the shrapnel in the doctored warhead would clean out quite a few of them.

Thumbing back the hammer, the Executioner aimed the rocket at the strike point of the Gypsy's tracers and pulled the trigger. The back blast of the RPG lit up his position, but the rocket flew true. In the flash of the warhead's detonation he could see that several Serbs were blown backward from the blast. He quickly loaded another rocket.

The second missile impacted on the flank of the Serb assault group, and again the flash of the detonation showed the shrapnel cutting a swath through them. The Serbs had gone to ground and although they were still firing their AK-47s, their assault had bogged down. Bolan knew that if the Gypsy could stay in action, they had a chance of breaking them up.

ON THE RIDGE LINE, Zhinkovitch saw that the attack had stalled in front of the machine-gun bunker. The RPG firing from the flank wasn't helping the situation, but it was the machine gun that was the main problem. If it could be taken out of action, his troops could move forward again.

"I want you to put your shells on that bunker," he ordered the mortar crew chief. "I want it destroyed."

"But our men are too close to it," the mortar man protested.

"You just shoot and let me worry about who gets killed. I want that machine gun taken out!"

"Yes, Chief."

Peering through his sights at his aiming stake, the mortar gunner spun the wheel that adjusted the tube's elevation. When he nodded, his assistant dropped the round into the tube.

EVEN OVER THE ROAR of small-arms fire, Bolan heard the cough of the mortar firing again.

When he saw the first mortar round detonate behind the machine-gun bunker, he realized what the warlord was up to. He was using the mortar to take out the only thing that was holding up the attack. Without close coordination between his mortar crew and his attacking force, though, Zhinkovitch was endangering his own men as much as he was the defenders. But clearly the man wanted the gun taken out of action, no matter what the cost to his troops.

His decision might have made sense in a different situation, Bolan had to admit, but not when the warlord had a limited number of troops to throw into the battle. His assault elements were too close to the target, and they were going to take casualties before the gunners could walk their rounds into the Gypsy's bunker.

As Bolan had predicted, the second round hit well in front of the bunker and off to the side. The gunners were bracketing the target to "walk" the rounds into it. It took five mortar rounds to do the job. Round number four hit the right front corner of the bunker while number five hit dead center on the roof. The explosion sent dirt and pieces of timber flying. When the smoke and dust cleared, Bolan saw that the roof had collapsed, but there was nothing he could do for the Gypsy. Until he could get the attack turned back, the small man was on his own.

One of the mortar rounds had hit the front of the fighting position next to the bunker, killing the two villagers manning it and creating a twenty-yard gap in the line. As soon as the mortar fire ceased, the Serbs charged the gap. For a long moment, there was no firing as the squads in the positions on either side held their fire for fear of hitting their comrades.

Bolan knew that he had to think fast. He hadn't had time to build a secondary defensive line for his team to fall back to, and as a result, the men stayed in their fighting positions, shooting at every Serb they could see running past them. But it wasn't enough. Two dozen Serbs made it through the perimeter, with nothing in front of them now but the unprotected village.

WITH A GREAT SHOUT, half of the reserve platoon broke out from behind one of the houses and charged the Serbs. Many of the old men and young boys had found bayonets to fit to their bolt-action rifles. Others had fashioned makeshift bayonets, using kitchen knives and sickle blades fastened to the rifle barrels. They were crude but effective.

The Serbs were forced to halt their advance and seek cover where they were. These villagers might not have been able to fight in the front line, but they weren't about to let the Serbs destroy their homes. Shouting encouragement to one another, they kept up a steady barrage of rifle fire as they advanced.

Suddenly a ragged volley slammed into the Serb's flank. Bolan saw Petrova and her second reserve unit, made up of the village's women armed with old bolt-action rifles, break out into the open. Petrova was firing her AK-47 from the hip on full-auto as she waved the others on.

Assaulted on two sides, the Serbs started falling back. They tried to withdraw, but the villagers were right on top of them. In seconds, it was a hand-to-hand fight with bayonets and rifle butts. The Serbs hadn't fixed their bayonets, and they found themselves at a major disadvantage.

Bolan saw one old woman swing her rifle at a Serb as though she were chasing a pig with a broom. The barrel connected with the gunman's head, and he went down. Another woman pointed her rifle and pulled the trigger. The round caught the Serb full in the chest.

Faced with the furious counterattack, the Serbs faltered. Following Bolan's directions, the villagers continued to shoot at them from every house corner and window, as well as from the flank positions along the perimeter. Unable to make headway, the gunmen started falling back.

"TELL THEM TO CEASE FIRE!" Bolan called out to Petrova.

When the firing stopped, the moans of the wounded could be heard. The attack had been turned back, but it was time to count up the butcher's bill. The first item was to see if the Gypsy had survived, as all that was left of the bunker was a pile of rubble.

"Let's get some men over to the bunker," Bolan told Petrova. "We have to get the Gypsy out."

Snatching up a shovel left by one of the work parties, Bolan started digging at the debris, a couple of villagers falling in beside him. Pulling a shattered timber aside, the Executioner saw the man lying over the breech of his gun.

He was unconscious and buried in rubble up to his hips, but at least he was alive. Grabbing him under the arms, Bolan pulled him clear and placed him on the ground. He didn't seem to have suffered any major injury, but Bolan saw that the side of his head and his arm were bleeding.

"Let's get him to the doctor!" Bolan ordered.

As two men carried the wounded man to Kubura, Bolan pulled the shattered timbers of the bunker roof aside to uncover the machine gun. The bipod was bent, and although the gun itself didn't appear to be damaged, it was out of action for the rest of the night. Trying to fire it when the feed mechanism was full of dirt was a good way to jam up the gas system so that it couldn't be fixed without a major rebuild.

BOLAN WAS LOADING ammunition into his empty AK-47 magazines when Petrova joined him.

"How have you been able to do what you have done for so many years?" she asked him. "I was so scared."

"You work through the fear like you did tonight," he replied.

"Does it ever get any easier?"

"Combat?"

"Yes," she replied, nodding.

"On the one hand it does, but the more experience you have, the more you realize how much can go wrong."

"The fear, though, does it ever go away?"

"No," Bolan said, "and that's good."

"What do you mean?"

"Fear helps you stay alive. It pumps adrenaline, which makes you more aware of what's going on around you, plus it makes you careful. A man without fear is a danger to himself and everyone else working with him. Only a fool tries to conquer fear. A wise man learns how to control it."

"So that's what you do," she said, frowning, "control your fear?"

Bolan nodded.

"How do you do that?"

Bolan smiled wryly, but said nothing for a long moment.

"It's not that easy to explain," he said finally. "Mostly it comes from wanting to do something more than wanting to give in to the fear. Look at these villagers. I'll bet that most of them were afraid. This is all very new to them. But despite their fear, they were determined not to let the Serbs defeat them. People always fight hardest for their homes."

For a long time, Petrova sat silently, then she turned to look at him, her eyes soft. "I—"

"Go to bed," Bolan interrupted her gently. "I'll keep an eye on things tonight, but I don't think they'll be back."

She sat where she was for a moment, before picking up her rifle and moving toward one of the huts.

Bolan knew that a close brush with death often left a person needing the comfort of another human. But he knew that this was not the time or the place. He still had a battle to fight.

19

The light of dawn showed Bolan how much damage had been done as a result of the mortar attack and ground assault. One house had taken a direct hit that had collapsed two of its walls, while another was little more than a gutted shell. He understood that even if the villagers won the battle in the end, their lives had irrevocably changed.

Worse than the damage to the houses were the human casualties. The mortar fire had killed three villagers and wounded several more, while the ground assault had claimed its own dead and wounded.

"How are they taking it?" Bolan asked Petrova.

She shrugged. "They are not talking about surrender, but I am sure that some of them are thinking about it. The mortar fire scared them very badly."

"Did you stop by the infirmary?"

"Yes. Kubura is holding up better than I thought he would. He has more patients than he can handle by himself, and Adan has given him some women to help out. The biggest problem is the lack of medical supplies."

"Speaking of patients, how is the Gypsy?"

"The doctor said that he is going to be—"

"Fine," the Gypsy interrupted her.

Bolan turned to see the man sporting bandages on his left arm and leg, and the side of his head. He was grinning, though, and his dagger was snug in his belt.

"You look a little worse for wear," Bolan said, "but better than I expected."

The small man shrugged off his injuries. "These are just scratches. I am ready to go back to killing Serbs and I need to know if my machine gun is all right."

"Your gun is intact. The bipod is bent and it needs a thorough cleaning before it's fired again, but it should work."

"Good. If you have nothing for me to do right now, I will see to getting it fixed." He looked out past the defenses. "I think we may need it again today."

"You'd better check the ammo supply. I don't think there's much left."

"I will make good use of what there is."

"He is a real fighter," Petrova said as the Gypsy walked away.

"I could use a whole platoon of him," Bolan agreed. "In the meantime, we'll need to repair the damage to the defenses. We'll use the rubble from the damaged houses to improve our fighting positions and build some barricades."

As BOLAN WALKED past the three captured Serbs, one of them called out to him. "Soldier," the man said in English, "can I talk to you?"

The Executioner turned to see an older, grizzled man. "My name is Lazar. I have been with Zhinkovitch for many years now, and I can tell you that he is not going to let any of you go free."

"Why do you say that?" Bolan asked.

"You have hurt his pride, soldier," Lazar answered, "and these villagers have made him look very bad. Dushan sees himself building a kingdom here like the old warriors did. In his mind, these people exist only to do what he tells them to."

"What do you suggest we do?"

"The only thing you can do is to take these people and run. You might be able to get away from him by hiding in the mountains. If you stay here, he will kill all of you."

Even though Bolan had figured that to be Zhinkovitch's intention, it was good to have his judgment confirmed. It didn't make the situation any better, but it made his way a little clearer.

"If he intends to kill all of us to soothe his pride, what do you think he's going to do to you? You allowed yourself to be captured," Bolan said.

Lazar looked him full in the face. "I hope that he will remember all the years that I have served him loyally."

Somehow Bolan didn't think that was going to be the case. "You had better hope that we win, then. At least the villagers will let you live."

By MIDMORNING, Bolan had a better idea of what he had left to work with. Their ammunition supply wasn't as bad as he had feared. Magazines salvaged from the enemy dead replaced much of the AK-47 ammunition that had been expended during the night. The only critical shortage was the 7.62 mm rimmed ammo for the machine gun. The Gypsy had burned most of it up during the night assault, and only about two hundred rounds remained.

He called Petrova over. "Tell the women with the Mosin-Nagant rifles that I need their ammunition for the machine gun. Issue them the old Mauser rifles instead. We have some 7.62 mm ammo for them.''

"They will not like that," Petrova said. "They are proud of what they did last night.''

"So am I, and I'll tell them so," Bolan said, "but we need to make the best use we can of our resources. The machine gun is critical, and I need to keep it going for as long as I can.''

"I will make them understand.''

Before Petrova took off, one of the village men walked up carrying what looked like an enhanced AK-47 assault rifle. It had a bipod, a longer barrel and a bigger stock than the assault rifle, while hanging from the action was a section of machine-gun ammo belt.

"I found this, soldier," the man said. "Can we use it?''

Bolan smiled. They sure as hell could. The weapon was a newer, Russian RPK squad light machine gun that fired the same ammunition as the AK-47s. Now, when the RP-46 gun ran out of ammunition, it wouldn't be so critical. Plus, if they couldn't find enough ammunition belts for it, standard AK-47 and AKM magazines could be used in it, as well.

"Damn right we can," he told the man through Petrova. "That's a good find.''

The man beamed.

"See if there are any more of those out there," Bolan continued, "and ammo belts. We need as many belts as we can find."

"I will tell the men."

No sooner had the man walked away when Bolan heard the cough of the mortar again. "Incoming!" he yelled.

This time everyone knew what to expect and immediately sought cover. The rain of deadly shells came faster, but they seemed to be concentrated on the defensive positions. Every fifth or sixth round, however, landed in the village proper, as if to remind the people that they weren't going to escape unharmed.

There was nothing for them to do but hug the ground and pray that the mortar rounds wouldn't score a direct hit.

FROM HIS COMMAND POST on the ridge line, Dushan Zhinkovitch watched the mortars pound the village below. He was rapidly using up all the ammunition he had for them, but he wouldn't back off now. In fact he had sent for the reserves he had stored at the fortress to insure he had enough to do the job.

This would leave his headquarters and base camp dangerously vulnerable if the Croats decided to attack him, but he had no choice. The villagers had to pay for what the soldier had put them up to, and they had to pay the full price. When he was finished with them, there would be nothing left of Valliskya except a smoking hole in the ground littered with corpses.

When this was all over, he would just have to raid one of the army supply points to restock his pile of ammunition, before his enemies tried to take advantage of his weakened position.

"Keep shooting!" he yelled to the gunners. "Keep shooting until they are all dead!"

The gun crews dropped their rounds into the smoking mortar tubes. Their chief had told them to destroy the village, and they would follow his orders to the letter.

THE GYPSY WAITED for the mortar barrage to end, his machine gun primed. He had gathered almost two hundred rounds from the reserve platoon and had reloaded his ammunition belts. Still, the four hundred rounds only amounted to a minute on sustained automatic fire, but in daylight, he could make sure that every round found a good home. After that, he would just have to wait and see.

He had to admit that the villagers were turning out to be better soldiers than he had thought.

In fact his opinion of them had gone up considerably since the night attack. If only they had more ammunition, they might be able to hold out against the warlord. But he knew how to count. He had seen how few magazines there were for the AK-47s. Even salvaging every last round from the Serb dead, there was still too little. They could make it through the day and maybe even the night, but it wouldn't last much longer than that. If something didn't happen to change the equation, they were doomed.

He had to agree with the American soldier that Dushan Zhinkovitch was the key player. If the Serb warlord was out of the picture, this battle wouldn't be taking place. His troops weren't real soldiers. Before he had given them their weapons and fitted them out in camouflage uniforms, they had been lowlifes, thugs and petty thieves. Without him standing over them, most of them would probably rather run than fight.

Maybe, if there was some way he could take out Zhinkovitch, then this whole thing would end.

ZHINKOVITCH STOOD next to the mortar tubes as the last of the 82 mm rounds were fired. That was the end of his ammunition and, for now, the end of the bombardment. It wasn't the end of the villagers' problems, however. He had just received word that the Croat incursions along his northern flank had been beaten off. With that threat taken care of, Zhinkovitch had recalled his troops to help with the final assault on Valliskya. He expected them by nightfall, and in the morning they would attack. A few hours thereafter, he would have the soldier nailed to a cross, helplessly watching the villagers dying before his eyes.

AFTER THE FINAL MORTAR round had fallen, the villagers came out of their foxholes, blinking from the dust and smoke that hung in the air.

Bolan surveyed the perimeter. Zhinkovitch had used his ammunition well this time. Most of it had been directed at the bunkers and fighting positions, damaging or destroying many of them. Few of the villagers had been seriously hurt, however, and the fighting positions could be rebuilt.

"Do you think he is out of mortar ammunition?" Petrova asked.

"For now he is, so we have to take advantage of that. We'll begin by rebuilding the bunkers."

20

The morning dawned cold and clear, and Bolan could see thin tendrils of smoke from the Serbs' camp fires across the valley.

The night had passed without another attack. Bolan had used the time to rebuild some of the bunkers and fighting positions that had been damaged in the mortar barrage. What the new day would bring was anyone's guess, but the big American knew that it wasn't over. If Lazar, the Serb prisoner who had talked to him, was correct, Zhinkovitch was only biding his time. And why not? He had everything going for him as long as he could keep his troops together.

Maybe what the villagers needed to do was to put pressure on Zhinkovitch's troops. Maybe he could send some of the hunters out to play sniper around the edges of the Serbs' camp. Bolan only had a few men to spare, but perhaps those few could do more good out there than they could waiting in the trenches for the next ground attack.

The warlord had lost men too, in fact considerably more than the villagers, and an outlaw band like his didn't take well to losing men. Maybe a few sniper rounds would go a long way to making the gunmen realize that they had little to fight for and a good chance of getting killed.

Psychological warfare was a double-edged sword that cut both ways.

BOLAN WAS GETTING an update from the village chief when Petrova came running up to them.

"They have captured the Gypsy."

With a start, Bolan realized that the small man had to have taken off on his own to try to take care of the warlord.

Bolan followed Petrova to the western edge of the perimeter and looked out over the trampled fields. Almost six hundred yards away, he saw a crude cross made of a tree trunk and what looked like a fence post attached for a crossbar. The Gypsy was tied to it. A broad splash of dark red marked his bare chest, and there was a gaping wound on his belly.

"He told me something last night and asked me to pass it onto you," Petrova said.

"What?"

"He told me to tell you that his name was Lando."

Bolan recalled the small man telling him that he would give him his name when this was all over. But it wasn't yet completely over, as the Executioner saw him move and knew that he was still alive.

"Soldier!" Zhinkovitch's voice came booming across the distance. "I have your man. He came into my camp and tried to kill me, but he was not good enough. None of you are good enough. I am going to kill each and every one of you this way. You are all going to take a long time to die."

The Serb stepped up to the cross. His hand flashed and the Gypsy screamed. Another splash of red appeared on his chest.

Zhinkovitch bellowed again. "I am going to kill you last of all, soldier, so you can watch the rest of them die."

Bolan knew there was one last thing he could do for the Gypsy. It was something he knew that the small man would do for him, were their situations reversed.

He turned to Petrova. "Go and see if the Gypsy left that long-barreled rifle behind," he said, "and bring it to me."

While she was gone, Bolan went to the machine-gun bunker and stripped two 7.62 mm rounds from the end of the ammunition belt. The Mosin-Nagant's internal magazine held five rounds, but he knew he would have only one good shot, two at the most. The black-painted tips on the bullets told him that they were what the Russians called heavy ball ammunition, a semi-armor-piercing round. He would have to compensate for the slightly heavier bullet weight when he took the shot.

Dr. Kubura had been drawn to the perimeter by Zhinkovitch's shouting. He found it almost impossible to believe what he was seeing. It was like something out of the Middle Ages, when men still fought barbaric religious wars.

Petrova returned with the rifle cradled in her arms. Bolan took it from her and opened the bolt to load the two rounds he had chosen. He shoved the two cartridges into the magazine and closed the bolt to chamber the first round.

The M-1891/30 Mosin-Nagant was one of the classic bolt-action rifles and had been used as a sniper's rifle for well over fifty years. Bolan would have liked to have had a telescopic scope, but the long-range iron sights would do almost as well.

"What are you going to do?" Kubura asked when he saw Bolan move over to one of the firing positions.

"I can't rescue him," the Executioner said, his voice grim, "but I can't leave him there."

"But you can't just kill him!" Kubura said.

"Do you want to see him die that way?"

Kubura shook his head as he stepped away.

Flipping up the rifle's sight, Bolan ran the range bar up to five hundred and fifty meters. He figured that the Gypsy was only a few paces over five hundred meters away, but since he was above the ground, the extra fifty meters would bring him right on target.

Resting the rifle's forestock on the packed earth parapet, Bolan settled the steel butt plate into the curve of his shoulder. He placed his right cheek against the top of the stock comb. A spot weld, as it was called, put his eye directly behind the aperture of the iron sight.

This was one shot that he could not miss.

FROM HIS POSITION on the cross, the Gypsy could see the soldier bring the rifle to bear on him. He didn't mind his death, as much as he minded the way it was happening. The Serb bastard hadn't even given him a chance to die like a man on his feet.

He could feel the sun drying the blood from the gashes on his chest. He could also feel the tug of his guts against the gaping sides of his wound.

He fixed his eyes on the American's distant figure. The soldier understood how a man should die.

The Gypsy slightly smiled and closed his eyes. His time was here.

BOLAN SUCKED in a deep breath, then slowly exhaled. One shot was all he had, two at the outside, and he had to make it good. He squeezed the trigger, and the rifle butt slammed into his shoulder as the 7.62 mm bullet went on its way.

A second later, the Gypsy jerked as the heavy slug tore through his chest. Then went limp, hanging by his wrists on the crossbar.

Bolan slowly took the rifle down from his shoulder. Of all the shots he had made in his long career as a marksman, it had been one of his best.

Behind him, he heard Petrova choke back a sob. Bolan said nothing. The Gypsy had been a good man and a brave ally. He deserved to be mourned.

ZHINKOVITCH STARED at the corpse. The single shot had struck the man right above the heart, killing him instantly. To make it even worse, the man's face held the trace of a mocking smile forever locked in death. The soldier had done it to him again.

"Attack! Attack!" Zhinkovitch bellowed. "I want to see every one of them dead!"

Snatching the pistol from his belt, he fired it into the air as he urged his men forward.

The Serb troops started toward the village at a slow run. Rather than hit the village's perimeter at only one point as they had done before, Zhinkovitch had split them into three sections. He had figured out the major weakness in the soldier's defense plan, and he was going to exploit it.

WATCHING THE SERBS FORM into their attack elements, Bolan knew that his sector defense strategy was going to be put to the test this time. He thought that he could handle two points of attack without much difficulty, but he wasn't sure about dealing with three. This was where the lack of radio communication—not being able to move his reserves where and when they were needed—was going to be a factor.

Bolan had anticipated this problem and had assigned some of the older boys to each sector to act as runners. If the attack in their sector got out of hand, they were to run into the village and get some of the reserve forces to reinforce the bunkers. It wasn't exactly a high-tech tactical communications system, but it had worked well enough in the low-tech trench warfare of World War I, and it was all they had.

"Let's get them in the trenches," Bolan said to Petrova. "This is it."

She didn't need to ask what he meant. She knew that this was the last assault. They would all live, or die, depending upon how well they fought. Checking to make sure that she still had the Tokarev pistol loaded and tucked into her belt, Petrova grabbed her AK-47 and went to alert the villagers.

21

This time, Zhinkovitch had no intention of staying at his ridge line observation post and watching through his field glasses while his troops attacked Valliskya. It was the last battle that would ever be fought in that miserable place, and he was going to make sure that it went the way he wanted it to. Also, he had to insure that the soldier was taken alive so that he could be made to watch all his filthy peasant friends die before his eyes. Any man who killed him would suffer impalement himself.

Mounting his stallion, the warlord slung an AK-47 over his shoulder and rode to the rear of his troops. "Move!" he shouted when he saw that they weren't going fast enough. "Now!"

The Serbs marched toward their objective. As they advanced, the village appeared deserted, but they knew that it wasn't. The embattled villagers were waiting for them in the trenches the soldier had shown them how to build, with their

AK-47s in their hands, ready to defend what was theirs.

Some of the Serbs had already discussed their leader's obsession with this small, isolated village. Usually when Zhinkovitch wanted to annex a village, all they needed to do was to show their weapons and the peasants cowered before them. Sometimes they had to kill a couple of the men to convince the people that they were serious, but never before had they had to fight this hard for a place this small. They had begun to wonder if it was going to be worth it in the end. Their chief had always taken good care of them and that was why they followed him. This time, though, he was getting them killed.

Keeping to the rear, Zhinkovitch rode his horse to within three hundred yards of the village before dismounting. Any closer and he would be too good a target. He knew that the soldier had fired the shot that had killed the prisoner, but there could well be other sharpshooters among them.

"Attack!" he yelled behind his advancing men. "Attack!"

PETROVA CROUCHED against the side of the house, her AK-47 clutched to her chest, and tried to remember what Bolan had told her about controlling fear.

Behind her, the reserve squads waited for the word from the soldier to go into battle. Their job was to stay under cover, out of the line of fire, but to be ready to plug any hole the Serbs might break in the perimeter.

Some of the men prayed while they waited, while others chain-smoked their homegrown tobacco and checked over their weapons. They knew that this was the final battle for Valliskya and that their future, as well as the future of their women and children, depended on what they did here today.

Vlady Adan was in charge of the women's reserve. They waited inside one of the houses, and would be sent into battle only as a last resort. Most of the women didn't like this plan. They wanted to be fighting beside their men—the same way they worked beside them in the fields. The soldier had spoken, though, and they would obey him.

In the infirmary, Kubura watched over the younger children. Bolan had offered him a rifle to guard his flock, but Kubura had refused. As he had explained, his refusal had nothing to do with his earlier pacifist beliefs, but with the fact that he had never fired a weapon before. For years he had been proud of being ignorant of firearms, but now he regretted that and the helplessness he felt as a result.

If he made it through the battle, Kubura vowed that he would learn how to shoot. Never again did he want to feel so helpless.

BOLAN KNEW that the only way to break up the assault was to take the Serbs under fire as soon as they came within range. The AK-47s weren't good long-range weapons beyond two hundred meters or so, but the old bolt-action rifles were. Not many of the villagers were as good marksmen as the Gypsy had been, but they could send rounds downrange, forcing the Serbs to deploy early.

He turned to the runner who had been assigned to him who spoke passable English. "Tell the men with the old rifles to start firing as soon as they can find a target. We need to break the troops up before they get in too close."

The runner took off, crouched over to make as small a target as possible.

A minute later, Bolan heard the rifles start to fire. A Serb gunman went down, and the rest of the troops hit the ground.

Even on their bellies, though, the Serbs continued to advance. One of the villagers in the western sector let his anxiety get the better of him and opened up with his AK-47 on full-auto. As if that were the signal, the whole sector opened up. Bolan didn't blame them. Even experienced troops, facing that kind of assault, would have itchy trigger fingers.

Now that the Serbs were engaged, Bolan knew it was time to use the last of his doctored RPG rounds. With the Serbs bunched up, they made a good target.

Picking up the rocket launcher, he shouldered it, sighted in on the gunmen and pulled the trigger.

The rocket arced over the battlefield and dropped into the middle of the attacking force. When the black smoke and dirt thrown up by the detonation had settled, Bolan saw that several of the Serbs were down, felled by the rocks and nails of the doctored warhead. He quickly loaded the last rocket into the muzzle of the launcher, sighted, then fired again. Putting the empty launcher aside, he took up his rifle, adding his carefully aimed fire to the defense. The replacement machine gunner was rapping out short bursts, raking the Serbs along a broad front.

The villager who had found the RPK light machine gun was following Bolan's instructions on how to use the weapon to its best advantage.

From his bunker, he rapped out short, controlled bursts, conserving both his ammunition and the barrel of the gun.

Rather than trying to storm the trenches in daylight, Bolan saw that the Serbs were trying to shoot it out from a distance. If they could gain fire superiority, they might be able to break through the perimeter.

Bolan knew that with their rapidly dwindling stocks of ammunition, the villagers would be defenseless before long.

WHILE ZHINKOVITCH'S FORCE seemed to be concentrated on the village's western sector, with him leading the assault, the attack from the south was looking like it was a feint. According to Bolan's reading of the situation, there were only half as many Serbs as there were in the two other groups, and they didn't seem to be trying to advance. Instead, they were engaging the defenders with long-range fire. The Executioner decided that he could risk weakening that sector. There were the reserves that he could throw in, to contain any breach.

"Go to the southern sector," Bolan instructed the runner on his return. "Tell them to pull every third man out of the line and send them over here to the western side."

Within minutes, the reinforcements started to arrive. They dropped into the trenches and began adding to the fire.

ZHINKOVITCH NOTICED that the volume of fire from the trenches was lessening. The villagers were obviously running out of ammunition. This was his chance to make the final assault.

"Attack now!" he bellowed over the roar of small-arms fire. "Forward!"

The Serbs charged the last hundred yards to the villagers' trenches, firing their rifles from the hip.

The villagers held their ground in the face of the assault. Although they poured fire into the ranks of the charging Serbs, it didn't seem to be making a dent in their numbers. Bolan fired well-aimed single shots at the lead ranks, but still they came on.

He understood this was the high-water mark. If the villagers could turn them back just once more, they would be able to hold on. Zhinkovitch's men had to be every bit as weary as the villagers were. They had been thrown back each time they had tried to take Valliskya, and they had very little to show for their efforts. If the Serbs were repulsed once again, they might break. And, if they broke, they might run. But it looked like they were going to need help to do that.

"Let's get the reserves!" Bolan shouted to his runner. "Tell Petrova to send half of them to the trenches and leave the other half behind the houses for fire support. Hurry!"

The boy dashed for the houses sheltering the reserves. Bullets snapped around him as he ran. The boy stumbled once, and Bolan thought he had taken a hit, but he got back to his feet.

Bolan jammed a full magazine into his rifle and flicked the selector switch to full-auto. Snapping out short 3-round bursts, he continued to sweep the front ranks.

If the reserves didn't get there in time, he knew the Serbs would break through.

22

When the Serbs closed in on the perimeter fighting positions, the villagers charged out of their foxholes to meet them head-on.

In a flash, almost a hundred men were muzzle to muzzle. When a magazine ran empty, guns were used as clubs. Bolan searched for targets in the melee, but it was almost impossible to shoot without hitting one of the villagers.

He saw a villager impale a Serb on his bayonet, but before the man could recover his weapon, he was clubbed over the head with a rifle butt. He fell, his bayonet still trapped in the Serb's body. Another villager took a hit, but he managed to blast his attacker at point-blank range with half a magazine of full-auto fire.

Despite fighting as hard as they could, the villagers were being pushed back, forced to give ground slowly, an inch at a time. Then suddenly the Serbs were through the line. A dozen or so of them charged forward, their AK-47s hammering.

But just as suddenly, the reserves were in place. Bolan had wanted half of them held back, but they all came in one bunch. They followed Bolan's example, driving into the enemy. AK-47s, Mosin-Nagants and old Mausers thundered, lashing the Serbs. The air grew thick with lead flying both ways, and while some of the villagers stopped a number of rounds, their surviving comrades didn't falter.

Three Serbs who formed the point of the attack fell to the concentrated fire. When another gunman went down to a well-placed round, they started backing out of the killing zone. When they drew even with the trenches again, they began to come under heavy fire from their flanks. It was more than they could take and they started to retreat.

Seeing the hated Serbs on the run, the villagers surged after them. For a moment, a storm of fire barraged the Serbs, and more of them fell.

When the surviving enemy troops reached the fire-support element of their force, their firing slackened. In the trenches, the villagers began to reduce their fire until the killing zone was almost silent, punctuated only by an occasional shot.

"SOLDIER!" ZHINKOVITCH called into the silence. "Let us call a truce and collect our wounded."

Bolan thought quickly. A truce would give the warlord time to get his men organized and re-supplied, but the villagers' supply of ammunition had to be almost exhausted. Bravery and determination wouldn't count for much, with no ammunition to back them up. Plus the wounded had to be attended to.

"Okay, Zhinkovitch," he shouted back. "Fifteen minutes."

As word of the cease-fire spread, exhausted and wounded villagers began to stagger out of their foxholes. The reserves moved into the trenches in their place.

"Soldier," the warlord called across the battlefield again, "we should settle this man to man. Come out here and fight me yourself. The victor will take everything."

Bolan looked around him. About half the villagers were still on their feet, but most of them were either out of ammunition or down to their last magazine. Even though a number of Serb gunmen had been killed or wounded, there were still enough of them to succeed in taking the village.

He knew that he would be taking an enormous risk. Even if he killed the warlord, there was no guarantee that he would not be killed by his Serbs. But it was now the only hope that the battered villagers had left. They had gone too far and done too much to have it end without him trying to make it turn out right. The last thing he could do was to take on Dushan Zhinkovitch.

"Zhinkovitch! Tell your men to hold their fire and I will come out," Bolan yelled back.

"No!" Petrova said, coming up behind him and grabbing his arm. "Do not go out there. You cannot trust him. He will kill you."

"I have to," he said. "It's the only thing I can do now to save these people." He looked past her to the villagers who had gathered to see his response. "It's our only chance. We're almost out of ammunition, and too many people have been killed or wounded. We can't fight much longer. If we give up now, it will all have been for nothing."

"Zhinkovitch's men are hurt, too," Petrova pointed out, "and they are low on ammunition, as well."

"I know," Bolan said. "That's why I think that if I can kill him, the rest of his army will fall apart."

Vlady Adan limped up to Bolan. The village chief was wearing a bandage on his left thigh and was carrying one of the bolt-action Mauser rifles. "You do not have to go out there, soldier," he said through Petrova. "We can still fight them."

Bolan admired the old man's courage. "Your people have done enough. I brought this on them originally and now it is my turn to see if I can get it stopped, once and for all. If I can kill Zhin-kovitch, it will all be over—his men have lost their taste for this. Keep everyone back here and make sure that they are ready to fight again if I do not make it. They have come too far to give up now.''

"We will be ready," Adan promised.

Stripping off his assault harness, Bolan took the AK-47 bayonet from its sheath and stuck it into his belt. He rubbed the palms of his hands in the dirt to get rid of any sweat, blood or weapon oil. He was ready.

With one last glance back at Petrova and the village, he started to walk toward the duel that awaited him.

As he crossed the battlefield, littered with spent cartridge cases, bodies and weapons, Bo-lan admitted that Zhinkovitch was a formidable opponent.

No matter how it turned out, it seemed a fit-ting way to end the battle. He owed Zhinkovitch for the Gypsy's death and for a lot of others.

PETROVA DROPPED the magazine in her AK-47 and saw that it had only two rounds left in it. "I need more ammunition," she said.

Someone handed her an AK-47 stripper clip with eight of the ten rounds left. Quickly strip-ping them into her magazine, she looked up. "I will need more."

Another man dropped the magazine from his AK-47 and gave it to her. She added the six cartridges to her own magazine. She now had half a magazine full, which should be enough for what she intended to do. Regardless of what Bolan had told her, if she could get a clear shot at Zhinkovitch, she was going to take it. No matter what happened to her afterward, it would feel good to kill him.

Snapping the magazine back into the well of her AK-47, she chambered a round and flicked the selector switch to semiauto. She walked out to the front of the perimeter, stopping when she had a clear view of the dueling ground. Taking a marksman's stance, she brought the rifle to her shoulder.

One way or the other, it was going to end soon.

It was just like Bolan had said. When you wanted to do something badly enough, it pushed the fear away. She had never been so unafraid in her life. She still feared for the American, but she was calm about her own fate. She was ready to do whatever had to be done to make this come out the right way. All that mattered was seeing Zhinkovitch's blood soaking into the dirt.

A HUNDRED YARDS from the village's perimeter, Bolan saw Zhinkovitch waiting for him. A dozen of his gunmen had formed a circle around him, their AK-47s cradled in their arms.

The circle parted to let Bolan through and then he was face-to-face with the Serb. The warlord had stripped off his embroidered vest and sash, but still wore his white shirt, black pants and high-topped boots.

"I am glad to see you, soldier," Zhinkovitch said. "Now we can settle this like men and then I can finish my business here."

"You seem to think that you're going to kill me," Bolan said.

The warlord laughed. "Of course I am going to kill you, soldier. And then I am going to take a long time killing that woman of yours."

"You seem to believe you're a great warrior, but you're really a coward and a bully, hiding behind simple, peace-loving people."

"You will pay for that, soldier," Zhinkovitch growled. "I promise you."

Bolan shrugged. "How many things can I pay for? I've already destroyed most of your so-called army. I've also shown these people that they don't have to submit to men like you."

The words were barely out of Bolan's mouth before the Serb rushed him, his curved dagger poised for a sweeping slash.

Bolan sidestepped the blade, but Zhinkovitch suddenly turned in midlunge, slashing sideways. The Executioner barely avoided being gutted.

He dropped into a defensive position, his bay-onet held out in front of him. For a man of his size, the Serb was blindingly quick. Bolan was going to have to be very careful. To underestimate the man's speed and strength would be fatal.

Zhinkovitch smiled as he sliced the air with the point of his curved dagger. "You do not show me much, soldier," he said sneeringly. "I was hoping for a little more of a fight. You should just fall on my blade and end it quickly."

"You talk again too much, Zhinkovitch," Bolan said.

The warlord snarled and charged again.

This time, Bolan was ready for the man's shift in midlunge. When it came, he countered with a side slash of his own, followed by a kick aimed at the Serb's knee. He missed his knee, but connected with his lower thigh instead. The slash of Bolan's bayonet, though, ripped through the sleeve of the warlord's shirt and scored. A red stain spread quickly over the white cloth.

"First blood," Bolan said, as he dropped back into a defensive stance.

With a cry of rage, Zhinkovitch was on him again, his dagger weaving like the tail of a rattlesnake.

23

From her vantage point in front of the perimeter, Petrova watched the deadly duel. She held the AK-47 ready, but with the two men circling each other and then darting in to attack, she hadn't been able to get a clear line of fire yet. Several of the villagers stood with her, their rifles also at the ready. If Zhinkovitch killed the soldier, he wouldn't live longer than the time it took for a 7.62 mm round to travel the distance from where they were and drill into his head.

When the villagers saw the splash of red appear on Zhinkovitch's shirtsleeve, something snapped in them. The warlord was human, after all. The soldier had drawn the Serb's blood, and if he could do it, then so could they. Many of them were out of ammunition, but they still had their rifle butts, their bayonets and, if it came down to it, their bare hands. After what they had been through, they weren't going to be slaves for any man.

Without anything being said, several of the villagers started forward, their AK-47s held at the ready and their faces set in grim determination. They marched on, crossing the open ground of no-man's-land purposefully.

When the Serb gunmen noticed them coming toward them, they snapped their weapons up, but with no clear directive coming from their leader, they hesitated to shoot.

More grim-faced villagers left their trenches and joined their comrades. They had fought a defensive battle for too long. It was time they got out of their foxholes and took the battle to their tormentors. No matter what the results of the duel were, they were going to eliminate the threat to their little village once and for all, or die in the attempt.

As the Serbs faced the villagers' hard eyes over unwavering muzzles, they realized that their leader had failed them. He had wasted too many of them in a fruitless battle, throwing them against prepared positions to be slaughtered. And now the soldier was beating him in a man-to-man battle. It was clear that Zhinkovitch's time was past. It was time for them to think about saving themselves. They began to lower their weapons and started to back away from the dueling circle.

Zhinkovitch saw the movement out of the corner of his eye and whirled on them. "Where are you going, you cowards?'' he bellowed. ''Stand and fight!''

Some of the men ignored him and continued to withdraw.

''It's over,'' Bolan said. ''You're history. Let's finish this, unless you want to surrender and go back to Sarajevo with me to stand trial.''

''I will never go as a prisoner,'' the warlord shouted. ''I will kill you, and my men will come back. I am their chief and they must obey me.''

''Give it up, Zhinkovitch. You're finished.''

With a scream of rage, Zhinkovitch charged, his knife poised for a gutting slash. Bolan ducked beneath the knife and delivered a thrust of his own, again drawing blood as the blade raked across the Serb's upper arm.

Zhinkovitch roared in pain and tried to close in on his adversary. As Bolan spun to get out of the way, his bad leg failed him and he stumbled.

The warlord stood over him in a flash, his dagger poised for a killing blow. Summoning every ounce of strength, Bolan thrust upward with his bayonet. At the same moment that he plunged the blade deep into the warlord's heart, Petrova had a clear shot and she fired.

The round struck the Serb low in the belly and he grunted as he fell back, Bolan's blade twisting in his chest. He tried to raise himself on one arm as he looked at Bolan. ''Who are you, soldier?'' he asked, the blood bubbling at the corners of his mouth.

Bolan didn't have to answer. The warlord convulsed once in death, then lay still.

For a long moment, there was only silence as both the villagers and the remaining Serbs stared at the body. Then, recognizing the grim look on the faces of the villagers surrounding them, the gunmen in the rear started stepping back even farther. Once they were in the clear, they began to run for their lives. In minutes, the only thing that could be seen of the late warlord's army were the backs of the Serbs making for the hills.

The villagers stood where they were for a while, absorbing the outcome. Bolan broke the silence.

''Are you all right?'' he asked Petrova, who had joined them.

''I am now,'' she said. ''It's over.''

Bolan glanced down at Zhinkovitch's body. ''Yes, it is.''

Two days later, Bolan and Petrova were ready to go back to Sarajevo. The dead had been buried, the weapons and ammunition collected and issued to the Valliskya Defense Force, as they now called themselves, and there was nothing more for them to do.

Vlady Adan headed the village send-off.

"I will report your situation to the UN," Bolan told him through Petrova. "I'll see if I can get them to send you relief supplies so you can rebuild and make it through the winter."

"We would appreciate that," Adan said, "but I know it may not do any good. Here the UN talks more that it does."

"You can never tell," Bolan replied. "With Dr. Kubura staying here, my President will be very interested in your village and he has a lot of influence."

"The interest of foreigners, even your President, has not always been good for us," Adan said. "Even with Dushan Zhinkovitch gone, others like him might try to move in."

"I will also see about getting a peacekeeping force to make sure that doesn't happen."

"That would be the best gift of all."

"You won't forget about the medical supplies," Kubura broke in. The doctor was unshaven and showed signs of not having had much sleep over the past couple of days, but he was in a good mood.

"I'm sure that I can get a medical team in here as soon as I get back to Sarajevo," Bolan replied. "I'm still certified by the WHO and now that I have the goods on the black-market smugglers, I should be able to get a chopper out here in just a couple of days. Plus, on the flight back, you'll be able to fly out the patients who need more treatment than you can give them here."

"I hope there won't be repercussions because I'm not going back, like the President wanted."

"It'll be okay," Bolan said. "I'll explain what happened. But I can't promise that he won't send someone else to try to talk you into going home."

Kubura smiled. "I am home, at least for the time being. I have a lot of work to do here, and as soon as I can get the medical supplies, I'm going to set up a proper unit. I suspect that Valliskya will be getting more refugees, and I want to be ready for them."

"I'll do what I can," Bolan promised.

Kubura extended his hand. "I learned a lot from you."

Mounting the horse one of the men was holding for him, Bolan looked over at Petrova, who was already mounted and waiting for him. "Are we ready to go?"

"Is anyone ready for a hundred-mile ride back to civilization on a horse? This animal will probably break me in two long before I get there."

Bolan gave a half smile. "You'll make it. You're a determined woman."

She smiled in return. "You're right. I will race you," she called out, digging her heels into the horse's flanks.

Bolan wheeled his horse around and raced after her. They had a long way to go.

**America is propelled toward
a deadly showdown in Cuba**

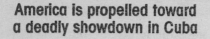
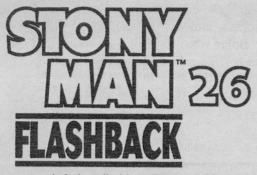

STONY MAN™ 26
FLASHBACK

Following a covert strategy that is nothing short of
treason, high-ranking U.S. military personnel are financing
Puerto Rican freedom fighters and Cuban hardliners to draw
Cuba into action that would expose her to a military strike.
Unless Stony Man can make a clean defensive sweep on
three fronts, America may face a nightmarish reenactment
of the Cuban Missile Crisis.

Available in January at your favorite retail outlet.

**A new warrior breed blazes
a trail to an uncertain future.**

JAMES AXLER

DEATH LANDS®

Bitter Fruit

In the nuclear-storm devastated Deathlands a warrior survivalist
deals with the serpent in a remote Garden of Eden.

Nature rules in the Deathlands, but man still destroys.

Humanity is headed for the bottom of the food chain and Remo smells something fishy.

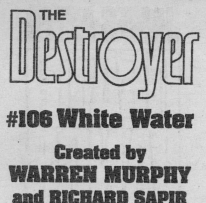

THE Destroyer

#106 White Water

Created by
WARREN MURPHY
and RICHARD SAPIR

Fish are mysteriously disappearing from the coastal waters of the United States, and it's anybody's guess what the problem is. Red tide, pollution? But soon angry fingers point north, to Canada, and the two countries trade threats and insults, all signs of neighborliness gone.

Look for it in February wherever Gold Eagle books are sold.